CLAIMING THE THRONE

THE DRAGON REALMS, BOOK 2

EVE NEWTON

Claiming the Throne

The Dragon Realms, Book 2: A Reverse Harem Fantasy

By Eve Newton

Exclusive to Amazon

Copyright © Eve Newton, 2019

This book is a work of fiction. Any references to historical events, real people, or real locales are used fictitiously. Other names, characters, places, and incidents are products of the author's imagination, and any resemblance to actual events or locales or persons, living or dead, is entirely coincidental. All rights reserved, including the right of reproduction in whole or in part in any form, stored in or introduced into a retrieval system, or transmitted, in any form, or by any means (electronic, mechanical, photocopying, recording, or otherwise), without the prior written permission of the copyright owner.

❀ Created with Vellum

1

~DELINDA~

I finally tear my eyes away from To'Kah. He is resting peacefully, so I am sure he is going to be just fine. Whatever magick Pres has packs a massive punch. I am impressed and intrigued that my little Beta husband has more to him than meets the eye.

"He will be fine," Pres whispers to me, stroking my foot and drawing my eyes to him at the end of the bed.

I am nestled between To'Kah and Rexus, both fast asleep, but I can't seem to shut my brain off.

"I know. You were amazing," I say with a soft smile. "Thank you." I crawl out from between the sleeping two and into his waiting arms. He is naked and ready for me. I am in a dark blue satin nightgown, which I slide up over my head so that I can feel his skin next to mine.

"Don't thank me, Delly," he says, slightly embarrassed. "I did what anyone would have."

"Well, not *anyone*," I spit at him, my anger flaring up at my family's actions. I am still so upset with Uncle D for doing this, but at the same time, I can't blame him. I did exactly what he didn't want me to do, and now everyone knows about it. If Papa hadn't been there…I can't even…

I choke back my sob and Pres gathers me to him, stroking my back, lest the Dragon decides it's rage-time.

"Your parents came through. Don't be too mad with them," he says.

"Humph," I mutter and then kiss him. "How did you get so good with healing?"

"My mother taught me," he says, looking away.

"Oh?" I say, sitting up. "Wow, she must be quite powerful."

"Was," he says shortly.

I feel like an ass. "Sorry," I mumble. "You've never mentioned your family…" I add hesitantly. Neither has Rexus. They know all of my dirty family laundry. It's time to learn about these men I am bound to. "Will you tell me?"

His eyes shoot back to mine. "Of course," he replies and takes my hand. He gets up off the bed and leads me to the fireplace. A fire is still flickering, so we make ourselves comfortable in front of it. He props himself up on his elbow as he stretches out next to me. I sit cross-legged, eager to hear what he has to say.

"You are so beautiful. More so, by firelight," he murmurs, his eyes bore into mine and his cock stirs.

"Later," I tut at him. "I need to hear about you."

He sighs. "My mother worked for your grandmother," he states out of the blue. "She was executed for treason twenty-two years ago."

"What?" I splutter, my hand reaching for his arm to squeeze.

He shrugs but says no more.

My mind is reeling. Grandmother killed his mother, and he is still here, *happy* to be here? Then a thought strikes me as odd. Or, at the very least, a coincidence. She was executed the year I was born. Something doesn't sit right with me about that, but I have no idea why. It just seems too strange.

"Does Uncle D know?" I ask.

"Yes, he was very apologetic and wishes me to regain my

family honor now that I am your husband. Take back my legacy."

"Jesus," I say. "And he told you this when?" I am suspicious now.

He narrows his eyes at me and offers me a slight smile. "The night I arrived."

"Oh, really," I drawl, folding my arms across my chest. "You his favorite or something?"

He shrugs, his smile getting wider. "Maybe."

I chuckle. "Well, I can't argue that you are one of *my* favorites."

"Music to my ears, wife," he says.

I bite the inside of my lip. His dominance is starting to show in tiny bits and I quite like it. I just hope it stays like this. I have enough Alpha maleness to deal with in the other two.

I glance at the bed, where they are still asleep.

"You know," he says. "This is the first time we have been alone, as it were."

I look back at him. "I want to hear about your family."

"Those stories aren't going anywhere. This moment will," he protests.

"Ha, well, you have me there," I say with a laugh and rise to my knees, giving him something to look at.

It lights a fire under his ass, and he is on his knees in record time, reaching for me. He tweaks my nipples and then pulls me to him to kiss me thoroughly.

I pull away and turn around so that he can cup my breasts and kiss my neck where I like it from him. He obliges me but dips his hands lower almost immediately to finger me. He finds my clit and flicks it gently, making me gasp.

"Mm, so wet already," he murmurs in my ear.

"Just for you," I whisper, in one of the few moments that I can say this to him.

He sighs with happiness and circles my clit slowly at first, building it up bit by bit.

"I love you," he whispers. "You don't have to say it to me, but I wanted you to know that I do."

"Oh, Pres," I breathe, shuffling back around to face him. I stroke his face. "I love you too. I knew it the second I saw you defending To'Kah."

His eyes cloud over and I realize that my words were perhaps not what he wanted to hear. But I needed him to know, regardless.

"I'll take it," he says lightly.

"No," I say forcefully. "It's not like that. I love you, Pres. How it happened has no bearing on how I feel."

He smiles then, reassured. He leans forward to kiss me again and lower me to the rug.

"This is so weird," he says after a moment. "I keep waiting for someone to take you from me." He chuckles so I know he isn't being serious about it.

"I am here just for you, my love," I whisper to him, before he plunges his tongue into my mouth at the same moment that he grips my hips and shoves his cock inside me.

"Sorry," he mumbles. "I just need you."

"I need you too," I say and let him pound into me for a few seconds before I turn us over and ride him slowly. He gently holds my breasts as they bounce with my movements, mesmerized by them.

"Gorgeous," he whispers. "So beautiful."

I preen at the compliment and ride him harder to his delight. I balance myself with my hands on his rock-hard chest, admiring the feel of his muscles as I work myself over his cock.

"Oh, fuck," he cries out softly as he comes inside me. "You just make that too easy."

I giggle. I love that I make him come undone so easily.

A rustle behind me, makes me stop my grinding and turn to look over my shoulder. "Hi," I say to Rex, who grins at me from where he is sitting, naked, on the side of the bed.

"Don't stop on my account," he says. "The kid could do with some alone time with you."

"Then why are you watching us?" I ask archly but adore him for his generosity.

"I have nowhere to go, besides, it's fucking hot. I like watching you." His dark tone makes me shiver in the best way.

"Thought you kept your room?" I ask anyway.

"I am not leaving. None of us are going anywhere," he states firmly with a look at To'Kah. "We will not split up. If we want you to ourselves for a bit, the others will just have to deal with it."

"I love you," I whisper to him and see him smile sexily at me before I turn back to Pres. "Can you ignore him?"

"Yes," Pres says with a laugh. "Especially as I agree with him."

"Good. Now see to me," I order and allow him to push us over so that he can start at my lips and work his way down to my aching clit.

Rex watches us, his breathing heavy, but he doesn't make a move to join in.

He will wait to be invited now and I intend to give him something to enjoy until Pres allows my Alpha to join us.

With a happy sigh, I arch my back so that Pres can take one of my nipples in his mouth as he twists the other one, just this side of painful.

I'm in heaven.

2

~REX~

I watch my wife writhing on the floor with her Beta husband. He is pleasing her well enough. She is enjoying it, and so am I. She is a delight to watch and so is he. I am itching to get my hands on him, but he isn't ready for it. One day he will be. He won't be able to stop the curiosity with us all being in such close quarters. He knows what I can do, and he will want to experience it. I can wait.

"Hey," I say to To'Kah softly as he stirs on the other side of the bed.

"Hey," he croaks out.

I lean over and hand him a glass of water from the nightstand.

His eyes immediately go to Delinda and Pres making love on the floor and he raises his eyebrow as he gulps his water down.

"You just going to sit there?" he asks me with a smirk.

"Uh-huh. This time," I add loudly.

I hear Delinda snicker.

"This is weird," he says and flops back on the bed.

"How do you feel?" I ask.

"Been better," he mumbles.

Yeah, I can imagine. I am confident his body is just fine.

After Pres kick started the healing process, with some fucking bad-ass magick that surprised us all, he healed up in no time. But his mind? That will be fractured for some time, I am certain.

"We—we are here for you," I say hesitantly, not knowing how he will take this. Or if he even wants it. As much as I used to know him, I am not so sure anymore.

Delinda and Pres stop what they are doing. I wave my hand at them to keep going. He needs this more than any of us.

Delinda is reluctant, but I think she gets that any input she has now will make him shy away, so she goes back to her lovemaking.

"I know," To'Kah says quietly, his eyes on Delinda, but then he grabs my hand and squeezes it tightly. "I'm fine," he says, drawing his eyes to mine with a look that tells me we will never speak of this again.

I nod and look down at our hands. I can't help the desire it lights up in me. I have wanted him in that way for a long time. He loosens his grip on me, but then surprises me by lacing our fingers together as he sits up.

"I'm taking a shower," he declares and lets go of me to stand up.

His bare ass, hard and sexy as fuck, makes me lick my lips, as he walks to the bathroom and quietly slips inside.

I debate with myself whether to follow him, and quickly decide that I will, helped along by the fact that Pres is now fucking our wife in the ass, his own clenched tight as he pounds her. I desperately want to make this an anal train, but I said I would stay out of it. So, I stand up and walk away, hearing Pres grunt with so much satisfaction, it makes me smile. He has definitely discovered what he likes.

I push open the bathroom door and see To'Kah step into the shower through the steam that is billowing up already.

He scowls at me, but then gives a resigned shrug. "I am fine," he says again.

"Didn't ask," I say, sitting on the rim of the tub.

"You have absolutely no boundaries, do you?"

"I'm afraid if you were looking for alone time, here is not the place. We are all here together now."

He sticks his head around the door, all wet and hot. "Not even in the shower? What happens when I want to take a dump?"

"Watching *that* isn't my thing," I say with a shrug.

He snorts with amusement. "Good," comes his muffled reply as he ducks back under the hot water. "So, are we just supposed to leave them to it?" he adds a few moments later.

"For now. The kid was a virgin before the other night. He had a baptism by fire. He deserves a bit of one-on-one with her."

"What?" To'Kah splutters, his head reappearing out of the spray, hair lathered up with shampoo. Delinda's probably. Fuck, now he is going to smell like her. "Are you serious?" He struggles to hold back his laugh, and it causes me to smirk at him.

"Completely. You wouldn't know it though. He has fallen into it quite well," I snicker.

"Hm, 'fallen into' the operative words there," he mumbles.

"Sore?" I must ask because there isn't room for it here. Not now. Not after what happened yesterday. We need to stick together.

"Not really. I know she loves me. It's just weird. I knew she was screwing around before. Obviously. But to see it, and be a part of it, will take some getting used to. I love her."

"So do I," I point out.

He glares at me and ducks back into the deluge. "It's different. I love her but I also love *Her*."

I pause at that. "Oh. Yeah, I guess I can see the difference."

"Can you? Because from where I'm standing, there is no definition with you."

My turn to glare at him, even though he can't see me. Asshat.

I stand up and rap on the shower door to get his attention.

He deliberately annoys me by rubbing his hand over the condensation to peer at me through the circle he made.

"I love her completely. I fell in love with all of her when I saw her Shift. Don't think you love her any better than I do."

"Oh, for fuck's sake," he mumbles at me. "Are we seriously going to get into a pissing contest about who loves her best?"

"You started it with your high and mighty attitude. Again."

"Sorry," he says, looking down and then disappearing. "I know I was a jackass and I am sorry."

"Fine," I grouse. "I'm not angry with you anymore. But don't give me shit. I won't stand for it and neither will she."

"Yeah," he says and turns off the shower.

He steps out, the water dripping down his body. I follow the drops down his washboard abs, my gaze lingering on his cock with a small smile tugging at my lips.

He is slow to pull on his towel, teasing me. It ignites the fire in me that had been on simmer while we talked with him just out of reach.

"Don't be a tease," I murmur, feeling my cock stirring. He sees it too and reaches for me.

I grab his wrist suddenly, twisting hard to get his fingers away from me. "If you go there, I want you all in," I growl at him.

"Who says I won't be?" he challenges me with a dark-eyed stare that makes my heart thump.

"You, several times in the past," I remind him.

He shrugs. "Shit changes." He yanks his arm free and stalks off, back into the bedroom. Over his shoulder, he calls, "Besides, it will make her happy."

I practically drool at these words. Fuck me. How the Hell am I supposed to stay away from him now?

3

~TO'KAH~

I smile to myself, knowing I have wound Rex up so tight; he won't know what to do with himself. I am game for it. I never used to be. But I never thought I would end up in a four-way relationship with Delinda either. I never dared to even think we would be anything except Guardian and True Heir. Like I said, shit changes. I sure have. Being as close to death as I was yesterday, puts things in perspective. In a big way.

Delinda wants me here and I intend to make sure that she knows that I worship and adore her, *and* her Dragon, every second of every day. I will do whatever it takes to make her happy and if that means letting Rex gets his hands on me, then fine. He knows what he is doing and won't make a complete fuck up of it. Pres is another story. I won't be anyone's trial run. Rex can take that on board, if he wants to, but not me. If I am going into this headfirst, I want someone who knows what the fuck to do because I sure as shit don't.

I throw the towel on the bed and walk over to where the love of my life is still being fucked by Pres, what did she call him? Oh, yeah, her Beta husband. I can't help the snort. It is definitely a pecking order. I wonder where I fit into this. Rex is the Alpha, but then I am no one's bitch, so where does that leave me?

I wait as Delinda shudders out a climax that leaves her breathless and then I drag Pres off her and dive into his place with gusto.

She laughs in delight and opens up her legs even wider for me, wrapping them around me as I sink into her, feeling the bliss that follows. It makes me feel good that I don't need to do anything to her to get her aroused. It's lazy and self-serving, and a definite plus to the multiple partners thing. Don't get me wrong, I enjoy riling her up, but sometimes my cock can't wait, and this is one of those times.

"Fuck," she cries as I slam into her so hard, I think I am going to break her in two.

I push down on her hips and pound her into the floor so hard, I know she will bruise. But she will heal up before we have finished, so it doesn't concern me, as it doesn't concern her. She takes me, all of me, and screams for more, her nails raking down my back, drawing blood.

"Delly," I cry out as I shoot my load into her at the same time as she clenches around me, milking every last drop out of me.

I hear Rex breathing deeply next to me and I roll off her, giving her to him. I am panting, and I need to watch him fuck her. The thought of it has my cock hard again within seconds.

I stare at him as he hands her a damp washcloth.

The look on her face makes me burst out laughing, but he says to her, "You are too slippery. I need a bit of friction to make this enjoyable."

"Jesus," I pant at him. "You have no shame."

"I want her to feel me," he pouts at me. "How can she do that when her pussy is full of cum and I'm sliding out of her all the time?"

She takes the cloth and proceeds to clean up, the smile on her face a wicked one.

She chucks it at me and then lets Rex take her. My cock is aching to be seen to, but I will let him have her for a moment.

It hits me suddenly that we are treating her too roughly and I sit up and pull Rex off her, just as he is coming.

"Fuck off," he growls at me, his cum spurting out onto Delinda's stomach.

"Wait," I say to him before he punches me. "We seem to have forgotten that she is pregnant. We shouldn't be so rough with her."

"I'm fine," she insists, but I shake my head at her.

"My child as well," I remind her.

"I know," she says huffily, avoiding my eyes.

I instantly become suspicious. "What is it?"

"Nothing," she says, getting up and walking over to the bathroom.

Okay, I know that evasive tactic. I just used it myself.

I am on my feet in seconds and taking her gently by the arm. "Delly?"

She turns to look at me, biting her lip. "Look, I had to do something. They were going to let you die," she adds vehemently.

I narrow my eyes at her. "What do you mean?" I drop my hand from her arm and take a step back as her look says it all. "You aren't pregnant, are you?"

"I don't know!" she wails at me. "I might be. The signs are there and we had sex right before my heat a couple of months ago. I needed my mother to believe it to save you, and she did."

"What?" Rex spits out, striding over and glaring at her. "You lied?"

"Not exactly!" she exclaims.

"Then what exactly?" I ask her calmly. I feel like my heart is breaking.

She takes in a sharp breath and folds her arms across her perfect tits. Her defensive stance.

"I thought that I might be pregnant before we had the talk

here yesterday. It's why I wanted to speak to my mother. So, she knew that the possibility was strong, but assumed it was simply very fast for us." She pauses to study Pres and Rex.

"But you knew you'd had sex with To'Kah during your heat," Rex states.

"Not during. Before," I correct him.

"*Right* before," she says. "By, like, five minutes. When I saw Uncle D about to throw you into the pit, I had to act fast. She brushed up against me and we both felt an electric shock. She said that was a sign for her. I said it was yours. But it might not be. I mean…" She gestures to the room, that, I guess, signifies the lots and lots of sex she has had over the last few days.

"You've only been with them a couple of days," I accuse her. "It cannot be one of theirs."

She shrugs. "They are my Chosen Ones," she mumbles, looking at the floor. "Who knows what's possible."

"It's a couple of days, Delly!" I protest. "That child is mine!"

"We'll see," she says and ducks into the bathroom, locking the door behind her in a useless maneuver, but making her point clear. Do. Not. Follow.

"Well?" Rex barks through the door at her. "It could be mine?"

"Or mine?" Pres gets in on the bellowing.

"It's mine!" I yell at them. "That is what everyone believes, and that everyone *has* to continue to believe." Don't they get it? I survived because of this. Remiel saved me so that his grandchild can have a father. No other reason.

It shuts them up and we all look at each other before Delinda opens the door and gives me a sad look.

"What are we going to do?" Pres asks into the silence.

4

~PRES~

"Good fucking question," Rex mumbles, he seems to have calmed down a bit.

I am still reeling from this news. I was prepared to accept this child on as my own but to have it *be* my own, wasn't something I had thought about. Delly claimed it was To'Kah's and Remiel saved him because of it. What if that isn't true at all? What if it is mine? Or Rex's?

"We agree that, for now, we go on as if this conversation never happened," Delinda says coldly.

I blink at her. I have never heard her use that tone before. She is deadly serious. Her face is a hard mask and her eyes are icy.

She has Astralled on a robe, so we all finally realize that we are standing around naked and do the same.

"For now?" Rex asks quietly. "How will we even know?"

She gives him a death stare, lifting her chin higher.

"It wasn't a slur, Princess," he says, rolling his eyes at her. "I mean it quite seriously though."

"I am sure that once the baby arrives, we can figure it out," she says derisively.

I am seeing a whole new side to her today, and I am not

sure I like it. This is the side that she needs to be Empress, I know that, but I want my lovely, beautiful, kind wife back.

"Agreed," I say quickly, so that she will stop looking at us like she hates us, and we can go back to how things were before this conversation.

She graces me with that gorgeous smile, and I give her one back, glad to be on her good side, again.

"Very well," Rex says stiffly, throwing her a tight smile.

I look at To'Kah. "Oh, you don't need me to agree. Fuck's sake," he mutters and turns his back on us.

"I'm sorry," Delinda says softly. "I had no choice. I was going to tell you. I needed a minute to figure out when and how."

"It's mine," he says, not looking at her. "You couldn't possibly know after a couple of days."

That seems to be his story, and he's sticking to it.

"Probably," she whispers, but we all know she isn't convinced.

I take in a deep breath and lead Delinda to the bed. "You need to rest."

She nods, her eyes on To'Kah. As she passes him, he grabs her hand and kisses it quickly before he drops it. She visibly relaxes.

"We need to start thinking about how I am going to claim this throne," she says in an abrupt change of subject. She sits down on the bed and I crawl up next to her.

"How exactly does that work?" I ask hesitantly. I am not up on royal protocol. "Does he just hand it off?"

She frowns. "I'm not really sure. We never got that far into discussing it. I assume so. I mean, it *is* rightly mine. If I want it, I should be able to have it."

"I think you'll find, that won't be the case. Especially now," Rex says, coming to sit close to her, and taking her hand.

"You have to take it from him, Delly," To'Kah says quietly. "It's the only way."

"Yes, I know that," she says to him, giving him a puzzled look.

He shakes his head and comes over to sit in front of her, his hands on her knees. "No, I mean you have to fight him for it. Kill him and the Power will transfer to you."

"WH—WHAT?" she splutters as I stare at him, dumbfounded. "Don't be ridiculous."

"That is how *he* got the Power from Tiamat. It is the only course, Delly."

"Why have you never mentioned this before?" she asks.

"You were never serious about claiming the throne before," he says matter-of-factly. "I saw no point in upsetting you until you were ready. I am guessing now, it won't be such a problem for you," he adds bitterly.

She blinks at him. "I know what he did was awful and wrong, but he is, nevertheless, my uncle. I can't *kill* him. And really, I *can't* kill him. He would smash me into the ground if I tried."

"He won't hurt you," To'Kah says, giving her an annoyed glare. "And he tried to kill me. You have forgiven him?"

"Yes," she says quietly. "I recognize that hurts you, and I am all kinds of mad with him, but he was upset with us. He trusted us and we disappointed him."

"Humph," he says rudely, clenching his jaw so tight I can hear his teeth crack.

"Delly," I say to her earnestly. "This can't be the only way." I know all too well what it is like to lose someone you are close to. Not to mention, I fear that if she goes down this path, it will ruin her.

"I'm afraid To'Kah is right," Rex says. "It's the sole way to transfer the Power."

"Then I won't take the Power, just the throne. I am already more Powerful than any other Dragon."

"Except him," I say lightly, to, you know, have something to say on this subject.

She grimaces at me and I feel my heart pound. I hate

disappointing her. It makes me paranoid that she doesn't want me anymore.

"He isn't likely to turn around and say I can't have it unless I kill him," she points out. "Also, he is my uncle. He won't hurt me to try to stop me from taking my rightful place."

"You hope," To'Kah mutters under his breath, but we all heard him, anyway.

"You cannot take the throne without taking the Power," Rex exclaims. "It makes no sense."

"It makes perfect sense to me," Delinda says, giving him a ferocious glare.

She has such fire. It is a massive turn on. I love that she could wipe us all off the face of the Realm, if she wanted to. Of course, I hope that she doesn't.

"I need to talk to him," she declares. "He will clear this up for me."

"Not now," I say, grabbing her hand to stop her from getting up. "He will still be angry after what happened only hours ago."

"Yes, but he was also explicit when he said I needed to get my shit together."

"Tomorrow, my love," Rex says. "Give him time to cool down."

She nods reluctantly. I think we all know that if we don't keep our eye on her at all times, she is going to Astral off to speak to him.

"Rest now. You have a baby to consider now," To'Kah says, giving the perfect reason for her to stay put and get some sleep. She can't refuse him.

She nods again, this time with more feeling and snuggles under the covers.

There is a slight rap on the door. We stare at each other, daring one another to go and answer it.

"Oh, I'll go," Rex huffs and storms off under a cloud to

yank the door open. "What?" he spits out and then goes quiet. "What do *you* want?"

Delinda looks up at his rude tone and we all try to peer around Rex to see who he is talking to, but he is standing solidly in the doorway, arms akimbo.

I have a sinking feeling in the pit of my stomach. I don't know where it came from, or why, but I feel that bad news is on the other side of Rex. We aren't left waiting long, when the visitor pushes past Rex and strides into the room, looking around. He jumps, startled, as he sees all of us sitting around in our robes.

5

~DELINDA~

I gape at the stranger that just barged into my room. I look between him and Rex and I feel like I have been punched in the gut. I blink once, twice, but no, the sight before me is still the same.

"You have a twin?" I bark at Rex. "Why didn't you say?"

He shrugs. "You didn't ask."

"Hey, Trey," To'Kah says with a nod and a shuffle closer to me.

"Trey?" I ask.

Rex heaves a massive sigh and says, very reluctantly, "Delinda, this is my brother, Trey'Za. Trey, this is my wife, Princess Delinda, and her other husband Pres. You know To'Kah, obviously."

"Uhm," the man who looks exactly like my husband says. He squints at me. "Wife? Other husband? What did I walk into here?"

"My bedroom," I snap at him. He is judging me, and it is pissing me off. "*Our* bedroom," I amend as I get three growls aimed at me.

He raises his eyebrow at me in a gesture so familiar to me already, I gulp.

"What are you doing here?" Rex asks him again, clearly

pissed off to have him here. I wonder why. Also, why did he never mention him, or any of his family? I guess, like Pres, we obviously haven't gotten around to it yet.

"I came to visit my big brother," he states. "They told me I could find you in here."

He puts his bag down and walks over to me, extending his hand out. "Princess. What an honor to meet you."

I glare at him in the most dignified way that I can, which isn't much considering I am lounging in my bed, covered only by a thin cotton robe. "There is a time and place for introductions," I say haughtily. "Now isn't it."

"Forgive me," he says, placing his hand over his heart and bowing his head. "I forgot protocol in the presence of such a bewitching creature."

I see To'Kah and Rex roll their eyes and I nip the inside of my lip.

"We will receive you later," I state dismissively.

Rex snorts. "That means get out." He points to the door.

"Understood," Trey says, backing away and picking his bag up off the floor. "We need to catch up, soon, Brother," he murmurs as he passes Rex on his way out.

Rex doesn't say anything; he just slams the door and turns with a face that just dares one of us to say anything.

Unfortunately for him, I dare. "A twin!" I exclaim. "How the fuck did that happen?" I didn't think it was possible to have twin pure-blood Dragons. They are hatched out of eggs, not grown in a womb.

"A short and uninteresting tale," Rex states, most unhappily.

"An irregular occurrence," Pres says very interestedly. "But not unheard of."

"Stop looking at me like I am an experiment to be studied," Rex snaps at him.

"Sorry," Pres says, sounding anything but. "I just...my mother said...she told me about you. You possess strong magick."

Rex gives him a withering stare. "Not really."

"Are you sure?"

"Obviously," comes back the irritated reply. "Now, can we drop this? Please." The last word comes out almost begging.

"I want to know more," I say. "About both of you. You and Pres, that is."

"Another time, Princess," he says, turning from me. "Right now, you need to sleep. You have had a trying few days."

Why do they keep trying to get me to sleep? It's getting beyond annoying now.

"I'm not tired."

"Tough. The baby needs you to take care of yourself."

Ergh! That is such a damn good reason, I can't argue with it. Fuckers. All of them.

I grunt, slide down further into the bed and pull the covers over my head. I feel To'Kah and Pres climb off the bed, so I make myself comfier. I might as well, now that I am here. I do feel sleepy now that I'm lying down and all is quiet around me. I feel myself start to drop off and let it wash over me.

6

~DELINDA~

I awake and it is pitch black outside. There is a small light on next to the bed, where To'Kah is stretched out, reading a book. Rex and Pres are nowhere to be found, as I glance around the room.

"Hi," I say softly, cuddling into him.

He gives me that sexy smile. "Hi. You should be sleeping. It's late."

"Can't. Where is everyone?"

"Rex went to speak to Trey and Pres is with your uncle." He grimaces at that.

I sit up. "I will speak to him. Make him apologize to you."

"No," he says, shaking his head. "I am not going to let it get in the way of us, and I definitely don't want you hating him over this. We will work it out. Just stay out of it."

I bite my lip, but nod. I am not sure that is the best way to go. I intend to have a quick word to Uncle D when we are okay again. I fear that may be some time though.

"Do you know why Pres is with him?"

"No idea," he replies and puts his book down as my stomach rumbles. "Hungry?" He smirks at me.

"Maybe a little," I admit as the gnawing hunger suddenly overwhelms me. "Come with me to find food?"

"Of course," he says and helps me off the bed. We pause to Astral on some clothes before heading out.

Deciding to walk, we open the door and head downstairs to the kitchen in silence. It is the first time I have left our room since the godawful events earlier. Everywhere is quiet.

Eerily so.

I can tell that To'Kah is keeping a watchful eye out, but I wonder if it's for me or him.

We have no idea what to expect from the rest of the Dragons when we do make an appearance in company.

"It will be fine," To'Kah murmurs to me, knowing exactly where my thoughts went.

"I hope so," I say fretfully.

He loops my arm through his and pulls me closer to him.

We walk on in silence and eventually make it to the kitchens without running into anyone at all.

I breathe out a sigh relief and push the door open. Knowing someone is in there, the second that I do. The light is on and two voices are arguing heatedly.

It comes to a stop when they see us hovering in the doorway.

"Rex?" I ask. "What's going on?"

He gives me a smile, but it is forced. "I knew you'd be hungry when you woke. I was making you something to eat."

"Bless you," I say to him with a big smile, and move further into the kitchen.

I warily eye up Trey, who is staring at me like I fell from the moon.

"Princess," he says as he sees me looking at him. "Is now a good time for introductions?" He approaches me, anyway, holding his hand out for me to take.

It would be rude to refuse him again, so I reach for him at the same time that Rex clamps his hand down on Trey's wrist.

But it's too late.

I have extended my own hand and Trey grabs it, squeezing gently as he bends over to kiss my knuckles.

I gasp as the shock reverberates up my arm in a bolt so fierce it almost makes me stumble back slightly.

What. The. Fuck.

I pull my hand out of his quickly and hold it to me as if I have been burned.

My eyes bore into Trey's.

He is smirking at me.

"I will leave you now to eat, Princess," he says and disappears so quickly, it makes my head spin.

I turn around so that Rex can't see the look on my face, but I feel the tension radiating off him.

A wave of nausea hits me hard in that moment. I place my hand to my mouth as the bile rises in my throat.

Of course this happened.

He is Rex's twin.

If Rex is my Chosen One, then that means that Trey is as well.

I make it to the trashcan just in time to retch into it.

To'Kah and Rex are by my side instantly, full of concern.

To'Kah hands me a glass of water as I straighten up and push my hair out of my face with a weak smile.

I have to look at Rex. I wonder if he knows.

Turning my eyes to his, I discover that he knows. He knew all along that this would happen.

He looks sick to his stomach and gives a slight shake of his head, asking me, no *begging*, me not to say anything.

I turn to To'Kah, but he doesn't seem to be any the wiser of what just happened between me and Trey.

Shit.

Fuck.

What the Hell am I expected to do now?

I can't have three Chosen Ones. Can I?

Judging from Rex's face, it is true, but he won't accept it for a second. To'Kah has suffered through a massive trauma and even the slightest change now will affect him, never mind being shoved even further back by another Chosen One. And

Pres will be gutted. Having Rex to deal with is one thing, but a carbon copy? No, he won't accept it either.

Jesus.

"I need to lie down," I mutter.

Rex grabs me and Astrals us straight back to our bedroom, with To'Kah following with food and water.

"Are you okay?" To'Kah asks me finally, giving me a suspicious look.

"Yeah," I say, grabbing the plate off him and preventing further comment by shoving a sandwich into my mouth.

"Trey made her feel ill. He has that effect on people," Rex comments, taking my elbow and steering me towards the sofa.

I sit gratefully and keep eating. I am starving and the nausea is abating now that I am shoveling food into my mouth at a rapid rate.

I avoid Rex's eyes for the rest of my dinner. But then I have to look at him. He hasn't taken his eyes off me. Neither has To'Kah, and it is unnerving me.

Fortunately, Pres decides to return at that moment, cutting the tension instantly.

"What did he want?" I ask him as soon as he has closed the door.

He is in high spirits, giving me a big beam as he drops to kiss me on the mouth.

"Just to discuss how best I can reclaim my family legacy," he says evasively.

It makes me wonder if he doesn't want Rex and To'Kah to know.

"Oh," I say, getting that he doesn't want to discuss it.

He nods and gives me a smile which then turns to a frown. "What's going on? What's happened?"

"Delly got a bit sick downstairs," To'Kah says. "And Rex had an argument with his brother. Not unsurprisingly," he adds with an eye roll.

"You don't get along?" I ask, needing to say something about this. Anything really.

"No," he says shortly. "I don't get on with any of my family."

"Why not?" I ask, intrigued.

"Now isn't the time to discuss this, Princess," he says stiffly.

I nod and give a shrug as if I don't really care. But I am dying to talk to him about this. All of this. If he really did know that Trey would also be my Chosen One, why did he keep it to himself?

7

~REX~

"I will run you a bath," I say to my wife. She is upset with me, any fool can see that, and I am aware of the reason why. She has figured out that Trey is also a Chosen One, and she thinks I kept it from her. I wasn't sure. I mean, I had an inkling. A very, very large one, but I wasn't one hundred percent sure.

I disappear into the bathroom and start to draw a bath, with bubbles and rose petals, plucked from the bunch I placed here after our wedding.

"Nice," she says from the doorway. "Trying too hard?"

Her sarcastic comment makes me chuckle. "Am I not allowed to be romantic?"

"I told you, I don't go in for that, so this has a deeper meaning," she points out.

Dammit. She can see straight through me. I don't like that. I am usually very hard to read. I perfected that a long time ago.

I duck around her and with a baleful glare at the other two men, shut the door and lock it.

I turn back to her and she has that perfect eyebrow raised at me, her arms folded.

"Get in," I say to her gruffly.

Her eyes tighten, but she does as I ask.

She sinks into the bubbles with a happy sigh. "You knew, didn't you? And you kept it from me."

"I didn't know exactly," I say truthfully.

"But you thought it might be true. That's not fair, Rex," she says.

"No, it isn't fair that he has this connection to you. You don't know him. We were forming a relationship of sorts before we knew for sure. And now he waltzes in here and you want him. Just like that."

I am hoping with everything that I have, that she tells me I am wrong about that.

She doesn't, and my heart breaks.

"I knew nothing about you or Pres and look how well this has turned out. You can't deny me, or him, this. You just can't."

"You are aware that I had trouble with sharing you," I growl at her. "I accept it now, but I didn't want to. And there was no way I was going to tolerate sharing you with *him*," I spit out.

She looks at me curiously, which then turns to annoyance. "That's not for you to decide."

"You are my wife," I say, hoping this will sway her.

It doesn't.

"Now that I know about him, I need to explore this."

"Absolutely not. I forbid it."

She gives me an imperious look that would have made me laugh had this not been deadly serious.

"You don't get to forbid me *anything*," she snarls at me, sitting up and exposing her tits to me. I can't help but look. They are exquisite covered in petals and bubbles.

"*This* I do," I tell her. "Not only for your sake, but for his. I can only assume that your uncle is still in a tizz over what happened earlier, for him to have gotten this far into the Fortress in the first place."

"What do you mean?" she asks suspiciously.

I sigh. She really doesn't seem to see. "This marriage between the three of us has just about been tolerated, because it turns out that we are both your Chosen Ones. Do you really think that your uncle, your *parents*, the rest of the Empire, are going to sit back and let another man make a claim to you? Regardless of the circumstances? To'Kah is safe for now because of the child, but do you really think Trey will be accepted?"

"If he is a Chosen One, he has to be," she states defiantly.

"And if he is quietly taken out before it becomes public knowledge?"

"That wouldn't happen," she says quietly, but I hear the doubt creeping in and pounce.

"They already know that I have a twin. You figured it out, so have they. Why did they not say anything? They don't want it for you. He spends every second that he can on Earth, and only comes back home, to Shes'Ti, when it becomes too dangerous for him to stay there any longer. They have been hoping he would stay away, but now that he is back…"

"You can't let them kill him!" she shrieks. "He is your brother. Your twin!"

I shrug. "I can't stop them." In fact, I can help it along. It will be a cold day in Hell before Trey ever gets his hands on my wife. I vowed a long time ago, that I will not let him take what's mine again. Ever. He can die before that happens, even if I have to be the one to do it. But a quick word in Dracul's ear will seal his fate. I have no doubt.

"If you allow that, then you are not the man I thought you were," she says caustically. "Furthermore, I will forever pine for him now that I know he is part of my destiny. Do you want that, Rex? Do you want me to be unhappy?"

Oh, she is nasty bitch. I'll give her that. But it doesn't change anything.

"You don't know him. You won't even know he is gone," I say nastily.

She shakes her head at me and sinks back into the bubbles. "We have a problem here."

"There is no problem if you let this go."

"How can I?"

"Because *I* am the one that loves you," I bark at her. "I am the one that you married and that has accepted your other men. I can give you everything you need, trust me on that, Delinda. You do not need him. And you will not want him if you ever find out more about him."

"What is that supposed to mean?" she asks.

"I refuse to continue this conversation, so let me make this very plain to you. If you decide to take him, you will lose me. Got it?" I stalk over to the door and yank it open, even though it was locked, and storm out of the bedroom, absolutely furious.

With Trey.

With her.

With myself for getting angry and giving her such an ultimatum.

I want to be confident that she will choose me, but I'm not. I have pushed her into a corner, and she won't stand for it. I need to go back and make it right.

I turn around, about to Astral off, when I see Dracul, talking with Aefre and Remiel. They are walking straight towards me and stop mid-conversation when they spot me.

Aefre gives me a frosty look that chills me, Remiel ignores me, but Dracul gives me a speculative glance that makes me know he knows Trey is here.

"Excuse me for a moment," he says to Delinda's parents. "I need a word with Rexus."

He doesn't wait for a response; he grabs me by the elbow and Astrals me off to his office.

"You know what I want to discuss?" he asks, folding his arms and glaring at me.

"Yes. Do whatever it takes to remove him from Delinda's

vicinity. I will not stop you." I feel no guilt, whatsoever, at my words.

Dracul's eyebrow goes up. "I see. You understand there is only one course of action that I can deem acceptable?"

"I can guess," I say dryly.

He aims a fierce stare at me for reminding him of the events of yesterday. "I will not allow Delinda to be drawn into another relationship. It is completely unacceptable."

"You don't need to explain it to me. We are completely on the same page."

"I find this reaction perturbing," he says bluntly. "Why are you so keen?"

"I love your niece. You are aware that I didn't want to share her, but I have accepted her choices. However, *this* I will not accept. It is out of the question that she gets involved with Trey."

"Does she know?"

"Unfortunately, yes. Trey got his hand on her before I could stop him. They both know," I say with a sigh.

"Great," he mutters under his breath. Then he gives me a penetrating look that chills me to my core. "I must keep my hands clean. I have already upset Delinda more than I ever wanted to with my actions yesterday. I stand by them," he growls at me as if sensing I was about to protest. "But I know it will take her some time to forgive me. I simply cannot risk losing her trust completely."

I blink at him. Should I tell him that she has already forgiven him? That she will now forgive him anything if she can forgive him throwing her lover into the fire pit to his death.

"What are you saying?" I ask. "That you want me to do it?"

"No," he snaps at me. "I would never ask you to do that, despite your…obvious…feelings on the subject."

I expect a judgy look, but I am surprised to find that there is only understanding in his eyes.

"To be frank, I don't want to know," I say, washing my hands of this. "I lost my brother a long time ago, as far as I am concerned, so do whatever you must, however you must do it."

"Very well," Dracul says with a nod, accepting my position on this.

I get that I am dismissed, so I leave without another word. Now, I must make things right with Delinda somehow. Perhaps a small deception would be in order. Now that I don't have to worry about Trey, I can be slightly less resistant to his presence here and in her life.

I Astral off to make peace with my wife, only to find an all-out war going on in our bedroom as I land, ducking out of the way of a vase that was thrown by my wife at her other husband.

He is furious, and it doesn't take a genius to figure out that Delinda has spilled the beans on Trey's status.

Fan-fucking-tastic.

8

~PRES~

I catch the vase that Delinda threw at my head and place it carefully on the dresser. I am inwardly raging at the news she has imparted upon To'Kah and me, but I am trying to remain calm so that I don't do, or say, something that I will later regret.

To'Kah, on the other hand, is telling her *exactly* what he thinks on the subject and he isn't holding back.

"How dare you!" she screeches at him.

"How dare *you*!" he yells back.

They both stop when they see that Rex has reappeared.

"And *you*!" she spits out at him.

She flies at him, talons drawn, but he catches her wrists before she gets a chance to slice into him.

To'Kah sweeps her up, his arms tight around her waist as she kicks and screams.

I stare at her wide-eyed. She is spectacularly mad. Fuck, she is gorgeous. She has a white and golden glow around her, which must have something to do with *her* Dragon, as I have never seen it before. It intrigues me and I move closer to her; She growls at me and I pause. I don't want those talons anywhere near me after She hurt me the other day.

"I'm sorry," Rex says.

"Oh, you will be when I get my hands on you!" she shrieks at him, kicking out viciously.

"I was upset and angry and I should never have given you an ultimatum. It was wrong and I apologize," he says, and he surprises me by dropping to his knees.

Delly stops lashing out and stares at him in disbelief for a moment before she regains her composure.

"Are you saying you take it back?" she asks stiffly.

He gives her an earnest look. "I take back the ultimatum."

"Grrrr," she growls at him, talons flashing again as she tries to get to him.

"Calm down, Delly," To'Kah murmurs to her.

"Fuck you," she snarls. "I haven't forgotten about you, just because he has come back."

"Princess," I say, trying to diffuse this situation, it has gotten way out of hand. "We are upset that you are trying to bring in someone else. We deserve better than a statement that you are doing it. It affects all of us. Not the least all… him." I gesture to Rex with my head. "Think about how this will be for him."

Rex shoots me a grateful smile which I ignore for now.

"Humph," she says. "You all need to think about how this will affect me, if I don't get him. He is also a Chosen One."

Rex growls at her.

"Oh, we are, make no mistake about that," I say to her. "I think we all need to calm down for a moment and discuss this rationally."

"Or, I can leave you all to discuss it while I go and make my claim!" She kicks To'Kah in the shin and he grunts in surprise and lets her go. She Astrals out before anyone can grab hold of her.

"Jesus!" To'Kah roars, hopping around, holding his shin. "What has gotten into her?"

"Let me go and talk to hear," Rex says, resigned.

"No. I'll go," I say. Rex will only piss her off further, I have no doubt.

"Fine but be quick. If she…" He goes pale and does not need to finish that sentence.

"She wouldn't," I whisper, but I don't feel all that confident.

I Astral out, straight to her side, so strong is our connection already.

She has her hand fisted, ready to rap on Rex's old bedroom door.

"Delly, don't do this," I plead with her, taking her hand so that she can't disappear again.

Her face softens, totally the opposite to the wild rage that consumed her only moments ago. "I need to see…"

"No, you don't. You have us. We will be everything you need. This will drive a wedge between you and Rexus. One that you may not come back from."

She looks down and I think I have her convinced, when the door opens and Trey grins at her.

"Princess," he exclaims. "Couldn't stay away?"

"Delly, please," I say again, and she looks desperately at me. Then without a word, she Astrals us back to our bedroom.

Rex is standing by the window, arms crossed and a grim-faced. He waits for her to speak, which she does after a beat.

"I'm sorry," she says. "I don't know what overcame me. I acted like a complete bitch."

His face softens, and he comes to her, taking her from me and hugging her fiercely. "Does that mean that you won't pursue this with him?" he asks tentatively.

She nods and gives To'Kah an apologetic look.

I sigh in relief that the tension has dropped in here and I tune out as they make up.

However, I'm not convinced. A few days ago, I would have taken her words as absolute, but now? I've seen a whole other side to her, and while I still love her, adore her even, I am starting to learn what she is capable of. I see now why Dracul needs someone positive to influence her. She is impulsive and has a temper to be reckoned with. I decide, in that moment, that this influence needs to be me. Rex and To'Kah are too hot-headed themselves. They are too ancient and arrogant; too jaded and have a dark view on the world. She needs more light, more laughs, more fun, and I know I can be the one to bring that to her.

I need to find the Emperor as soon as I can to ask his advice on how best to handle her. She will see it coming from a mile away if I try to sway her with words. This needs smooth moves, something I am pretty sure I don't possess.

"Pres?" she calls to me.

I look up to see that she is already naked and waiting for me to join them on the bed.

I waste no time. I ache to be inside her. Finding Dracul, will just have to wait.

9

~TO'KAH~

I'm a greedy son-of-a-bitch, but I don't care. Now that I am free to be with Delinda, I just need to be with her all of the time. Touching her. Kissing her. Biting her ripe nipples. Sliding into her wet pussy. Thrusting. Pounding.

"Fuck," I breathe out as I come again inside her, shooting my load deep into her, as I push her hips into the bed. "I need to do it again."

"Erm," Rex says, tapping me on the shoulder. "You've been there through three of your own orgasms. I suggest giving someone else a chance."

"Can't. Help. It," I pant as I speed up again, already rock-hard and needing a release. "Need her."

"So do we," he mutters.

She giggles underneath me. "One more and then you have to share," she says.

"Done," I pant, slamming my hips against her. I feel her clench around me for the fifth time. She is fucking amazing. She feels like heaven and I never want to leave her. "Oh, Delly."

She squeezes my ass hard and wraps her legs around me. I know she is going to roll us over so that her body is accessible to the other two men. That's fine. I am inside her and that's all I care about right now.

She does as I expect, and they are on her in the next second. Tweaking her nipples. Kissing her. Ravaging her body with their hands and mouths.

"Yes," I pant as she rides me harder and harder. "Perfect. Just perfect." I groan as I come again so quickly, I didn't get a chance to make sure she did as well.

She slows the movement of her hips, riding me slowly through what feels like a never-ending climax. My balls are so tight. My heart is pounding. There is a fire in my veins.

Then she is gone.

Lifted off me by her Alpha husband who slams into her so hard, the bed rocks under the force of it.

She laughs, but she loves it. "Easy, tiger," she chuckles at him. "I will always be here."

"Thank fuck for that," Rex grunts, coming inside her already. "Not enough. I need more."

"I have more than one hole," she says, making us all groan in response.

Since we found out that she is pregnant, we have taken her one at a time, not wanting to hurt her or the baby.

Now that she is giving us the go ahead, we don't fail to comply.

We intend on filling all of her holes at once, and I want her hot tongue wrapped around my cock so that I can come in her mouth and have her swallow it.

Rex falls back to the bed with her on top of him, giving Pres access to her ass. It seems to be his thing. He eagerly gets into position, delving his fingers into her dripping pussy to lube up her ass before he drills her so hard, she screams.

Rex is back inside her the second Pres's fingers are out and together they rock her almost off the bed.

She screams with ecstasy while I climb off the bed and watch her for a moment, her nipples so tight they appear ready to pop. I reach out and flick one before I suck it into my mouth, grinding my teeth around it gently making her moan.

"I love you," she whispers, her eyes closed against this onslaught.

"I love you," I say to her before I stand up straight and position my cock at her mouth. She opens like a good girl and sucks me so hard I am about to burst again. No woman has ever done this to me before. I expect that no woman ever could. Not that I will try to find out. I am in this completely and I won't ever let her go now that I have her.

Her tongue slides down my length, her teeth gliding over me gently, her lips working their way up and down. Her hand joins her mouth, and it's too much. My cum floods her mouth as I roar with desire, gripping the back of her head to make sure she takes it all.

She pops her mouth off me and swallows, licking her lips and firing up my engines again.

Fuck. How does she do this to me?

I am about to rearrange this jumble of bodies, when Rex's hand slides up my leg to cup my balls. I freeze, but Delinda's eyes go so wide with desire, it instantly makes me relax. She wants to see this.

Pres pants as he comes in her ass and shortly after pulls out, watching this with interest on his face.

Delinda moves her hips now that she isn't impaled from both ends, riling Rex up, but he is looking at me.

I grab Rex by the wrist to move his hand to my cock.

His eyes burn with desire as he grips me hard and starts to tug.

Delinda moans and comes as she watches Rex's hand.

"Oh, fuck," she rasps, putting her hands on Rex's chest, slowing her movements until she stops.

"Don't stop," Rex murmurs to her. "I want to feel you fucking me as I suck him off."

"Uhhh," she groans and speeds up again, letting Rex sit up.

"You all in?" he murmurs to me.

"Yes," I say, keeping my eyes on Delinda. I can do this because I want to see *her* reaction, not Rex's.

I move even closer so that Rex's mouth has access to me.

Delinda pants, her eyes swimming with raw lust as Rex opens up and takes my rock-hard cock in his mouth.

"Holy Hell," she breathes.

Pres has moved in behind her to grab her tits and tweak her nipples, playing with them, but keeping his eyes on me and Rex.

"More," Delinda pants. "More."

Rex obliges her with a wicked look up at me.

He gives me, what I have to say, is a fucking fine blow job. He definitely knows what he is doing and I'm glad. If we were fumbling our way through this, it wouldn't be as sexy as I am sure it is now, judging from Delly's reaction. I keep my eyes on hers as I feel the climax building inside me.

"I'm close," I murmur to her, but letting Rex know so that he can decide if he is going to let me come in his mouth or pull away.

He doesn't go anywhere, in fact he sucks harder, working his tongue over my cock until I feel my balls tighten, and I shoot my load into his mouth.

"Fuck. Fuck. Fuck!" Delinda cries as she comes again round Rex's dick.

He swallows and comes inside her at the same time, with a guttural moan that makes me twitch in his mouth.

"Oh, the gods," Delly whispers, her eyes roving over us with such hunger. "I need to see more. Will you?" she asks me, clearly already knowing Rex's feelings about this.

I nod, a bit nervous now. A blow job is one thing, but what is he going to want me to do next?

Pres is breathing heavily, having taken himself in his hand to jerk off, while he watches us. Delly pulls her eyes away from us and drops her head lower to take him in her mouth so that he can come in hot bursts down her throat.

"I want to see more," he croaks out.

Rex takes Delinda and lifts her off him, rising to his knees to face me. His eyes are challenging me to refuse him when he leans forward, his hand on the back of my head, to press his lips to mine.

"Taste yourself," he murmurs before he plunges his tongue into my mouth.

"Oooh," Delinda moans, grabbing Pres and slamming him back to the bed right next to us. She straddles him, pushing his cock inside her as she watches.

It makes my cock so hard; I am ready to burst yet again. She is using us as her own personal porn and it is so arousing, I let out a loud moan.

Rex pulls back from our kiss and I tear my eyes away from Delinda to look into their dark depths. "Do you want me to fuck you?" he asks me quietly.

I look back at Delinda. Her eyes are wide, her fingers on her clit as she coaxes herself to an orgasm. She might be using Pres's cock to fuck her, but she is thinking only about us.

I turn back to Rex.

"Yes."

10

~REX~

I give To'Kah a slow smile after he has given me his consent to take his body and make it mine, before I give him back to my wife to appease his need for a woman.

I have waited for this moment for a remarkably long time. I am over a thousand years old. I learned a long time ago that I didn't really care about pussies or dicks. If I found someone attractive, that was it for me.

To'Kah and I have been friends for hundreds of years, long before the Queen was discovered and tore us apart. I knew the second that I saw him, back on Earth, that I wanted him. He made it clear, as soon as he knew, that it wasn't going to happen. Yet, here we are.

I focus solely on him. I don't want to watch Delinda's reaction to this. Not yet. I will wait until I am riding his ass to look at her face. She will be so turned on by it, it makes my cock twitch. To'Kah feels it and looks down, grabbing it and jerking me off gently as he gets used to the feel of a cock in his hand that isn't his own.

"Don't be afraid, you won't hurt me," I murmur to him, brushing his long hair off his face. It has fallen in a black silk curtain, that I am sure he did on purpose to hide behind.

But I want to see him. I want my wife to see him. I want

her other husband to see him. I want Pres to see exactly what I do to To'Kah and how it makes him feel so that when the time comes, he will be ready for me to do it to him.

I groan and throw my head back as To'Kah takes me at my word and speeds up his movements, his hand tugging me roughly now. My balls are so tight, but I don't want to come in his hand.

"Please," I hear Delinda whimper and it makes me push To'Kah's hand away. She wants the main event and I want to give that to her, just as much as I want it for myself.

I frown and blink at her.

She knows my thoughts and bites her lip. Then, her face lights up and she jumps off the bed and Astrals to the bathroom and back to the bedroom in a few seconds.

She wordlessly hands me a small tin and climbs back on Pres to carry on fucking him while she watches us.

I glance at the tin on my palm and smile. It is a tiny tin of Vaseline, used as lip balm.

I grin at her and pop the top. She catches her breath, as does To'Kah.

"I want to take you in the ass," Pres murmurs to her. "At the same time."

My heart pounds at his words. I want that as well.

She climbs off him and they arrange themselves, adjacent to us, but I leave them to it.

My eyes bore into To'Kah's. He is staring right back at me, almost daring me to give him an out.

I laugh. "Don't think so," I whisper to him and drop my mouth to his to kiss him again, my hand wrapping around his cock to bring him to attention.

He is already like iron, so I don't have to work too hard, which is good news. It means he really wants this.

He kisses me back, in a damn fine swirl of tongues that I am reluctant to pull away from. "Turn around," I say hoarsely, suddenly feeling a bit nervous now myself. It's completely out of the blue. I have done this a million times, just not with someone I cared so much about. If I hurt him, or turn him off, or he decides this isn't for him, it will ruin us.

I watch him as he positions himself on his hands and knees, gripping the dark green coverlet tightly.

Delinda is in the same position, already being fucked in her ass slowly. She reaches out and grabs To'Kah's hand, squeezing it and then lacing her fingers through his. It is awkward for them both, but his knuckles go white, he is gripping her hand so tightly.

I stick my finger in the tin and scoop up half of it on the tip. I discard it and place my other hand on To'Kah's ass. He tenses up, but Delinda whispers to him to relax.

He does exactly as she asks, which makes the tension leave my body as well.

I reach down and lube up To'Kah's ass slowly. I circle the hole and then insert my finger just a little bit before I withdraw and proceed to do it again, getting him used to the invasion, a bit at a time, until my finger is inside his ass up to the knuckle.

He is breathing deeply and evenly as if to calm himself, so I decide to get on with it. I want to play with him a bit more, but he needs me to do it now.

"Ready?" I ask quietly.

"Yes," he replies.

The only sound after that, is Pres's grunts as he fucks our wife and her moans of desire as she lifts her head up to look at me.

I pin her eyes as I grab To'Kah's ass and press my tip to the hole.

I slowly push forward, finding resistance, but needing to break through it.

He grunts as he yields for me and then he relaxes completely. The hardest bit is over with and now he can enjoy what I will give him.

I keep pushing forward slowly until I am balls deep in his

ass and I groan. I allow myself to feel how tight he is, how utterly enthralling it is to take his virgin ass and make it mine.

"Fuck," Pres cries out and shoots his load into Delinda's ass before I have even got started.

She shudders as well, having brought her hand up to play with her clit as she watched me enter her lover. Pres grabs the ever-handy washcloth and cleans up, clearly expecting more than just an ass fucking from his wife.

"You are gorgeous," she breathes. "Now fuck him."

I chuckle at the order, and so does To'Kah. I have no problem with complying with it. I start to move my hips, drawing my cock out slightly and then thrusting back in.

He starts to moan. Delinda snakes her hand underneath him, to pump at his cock as I pound his ass.

"Fuck," he rasps. "Fuck. Harder."

"Which one?" Delinda asks wickedly.

"Both," he croaks out. "Fuck me harder, both of you."

"Uhn," Pres chokes out a noise of raw lust that makes my cock twitch and my balls tighten.

He shuffles across the bed to kneel in front of To'Kah, his cock in his hand. "Please," he begs.

"Oh, yes," Delinda moans. "Yes."

I watch as To'Kah hesitates for a second before he opens his mouth to take Pres in. Pres wastes no time in moving his hips, fucking To'Kah's mouth, taking all of the control. It makes me grin at him, but his eyes are closed in ecstasy. I go back to my task, making sure to fuck To'Kah harder and harder with each thrust. He is grunting with the effort of every part of him being seen to.

I feel him tense up and then let out a guttural moan as he comes in Delinda's hand. Pres follows in his mouth shortly afterwards, so that leaves me. I am close, really close. I slam my hips against To'Kah, my hands gripping him tightly and that's when my orgasm hits me in a vortex of pure bliss. The heat races through me as my seed shoots into him. I shudder as I unload so much cum into him, I think it is never going to end. My groan is muffled by Delinda's mouth on mine, kissing me fiercely, her hand tight around my throat.

Then it is over.

I pull my cock out of To'Kah's ass and slap him lightly. "Take her now," I rasp, my voice hoarse with the overwhelming emotion that has flooded me. I have fallen completely in love with my best friend. I always knew it was possible; the feelings were always there, simmering under the surface, but kept at bay to save myself the pain of rejection. But now that he has let me make love to him, I allow the feelings to take me, to sweep me up in the sheer force of it.

I wonder how I got so lucky to be in love with not only the woman of my dreams, but the man as well.

11

~DELINDA~

"That's it, baby, fuck me hard," I pant as To'Kah is hellbent on breaking me in two, it seems. My husbands leave us alone while To'Kah takes me, knowing that he needs this after everything that just happened. I am surprised he took it so well, and I am deeply, *frighteningly*, more in love with him than I ever was. I know he did this for me. For me to enjoy watching, but I also know that he enjoyed it. A lot. He was rock-hard when I grabbed his cock to make him come. He probably would have gotten there on his own, which makes me very happy.

Then Pres joined in and I have never felt so turned on in my life.

I clench around To'Kah almost immediately, milking him, needing him to just let go, which he does, spurting his cum inside my dripping wet pussy. He slides out because I am so drenched with cum, but I don't care. I feel so loved and so happy, I could stay like this forever.

To'Kah rolls off me and instantly falls asleep. I smirk at him and then turn to my two husbands.

"Thank you," I whisper. "That was…amazing." I stretch like a contented cat, and let out a big, noisy yawn.

They both chuckle at me and get me cleaned up and

tucked up in bed. "At this rate, you will spend most of your time resting, Princess. We need to give you some time where we *don't* fuck," Rex says.

"What?" I exclaim, sitting back up. "No way. I don't like that idea."

Rex pushes me back down and tucks me up again. "Warms my heart, little Dragon. Now rest." He gives me a sweet kiss, followed by Pres, who is looking a little shy after his exploits earlier.

"I couldn't help myself," he whispers against my lips.

"I'm glad. It was fucking hot."

He goes bright red and then climbs onto the bed to snuggle into me and falls asleep right away as well. That leaves Rex, who settles on the foot of the bed.

I soon drift off, surrounded by my men, happy and full of positive vibes. Everything will work out. I just know it.

I awake sometime later to a soft knock on the door. The men are all still fast asleep, so I get up and Astral on my robe. I open the door and peek through it, to see my parents standing there.

"What?" I hiss at them.

"Delinda," Papa warns me.

I shoot him a mutinous glare, but I try to adjust my attitude as I drop the defensive stance and glance back to the bed.

Mother follows my gaze and sees the pile of sleeping men on my bed and she cringes. It's probably one thing to know that your daughter is shacking up with three men, but to see it is a whole other bag. Let me assure you, the same can be said for your mother.

"We'll talk out here," I say and move forward, so they have to fall back or get shoved out of the way. I close the door and look at them.

"Well?"

"Delly, please, we know you are upset about what happened. Rest assured your uncle is feeling bad about his actions, but you need to listen to what we have to tell you," Mother says.

"Okay," I say and wait.

She bites her lip and glances again at Papa. He is no help. I would giggle if I weren't so furious with them both. She shakes her head at him and looks back at me. "You need to take control of this Empire, sooner rather than later," she whispers to me.

I give her a scathing look. "You don't say," I drawl.

"I know you think it is because of what happened earlier, but this is about something else. Your uncle is growing impatient, and he is going to fix this to his liking if you don't fall in line."

That grabs my full attention. "What do you mean?" I ask with a frown.

"It means, that he will use his resources and change things," she says cryptically.

"I see," I say, even though I don't. I haven't got an inkling what she means. "Well, we have already decided that I can no longer run from my destiny. We are going to make sure that I am ready to take control as soon as possible."

She nods slowly. "You are all on the same page?" she asks delicatcly.

"Of course," I scoff. "We are in this together. Even more so now after the attempted execution of my child's father." I give her an icy glare.

"About that…" she starts, but I hold my hand up to stop her.

"I'm grateful that you eventually put an end to that madness, but I cannot forget that you wanted him dead in the first place. It will take me some time to get over this betrayal," I say and then sweep back into my room, shutting the door on them with a soft thump.

"What did they want?" Rex asks me quietly.

He has gotten dressed in loose sweats and a vest. I nearly drool when I peer at him. He is so good-looking it makes me wet just looking at him. Don't even get me started on all the things he did earlier.

"Just to apologize," I say with a shrug. I say the white lie easily as it is more of an omission to not tell him about the other part. Something doesn't sit right with me about that, and I would rather not get my men in a tizzy over it.

He nods, accepting it and then takes my hand and brings me to the bathroom. "I'll draw you a bath and then you need to eat. We are distracting you too much and it has to end. You need to look after yourself. No, *we* need to look after you and our baby."

"I don't want it to end," I pout at him. "I adore making love to you all the time. Especially when it ends up like today."

"Hmm, me too," he says, his eyes going darker at the memory. "About that…" He walks past me to drop the toilet seat back into place and closing the lid so I can sit. He perches on the bath and takes my hands when I lower myself to this proverbial chair. "I need to say something to you about To'Kah."

"You are in love with him," I state, already knowing that is what he wants to say. I could see it on his face after he finished making love with To'Kah. And that is exactly what it was: making love.

"Yes," he says, with a nod and a grim look on his face. "I am."

I lick my lips and decide if I can say what is bothering me about that.

"Listen to me before you say, or think, anything else," he urges me.

"Okay," I say warily.

"I am in love with him, as I am in love with you. But I am *your* husband. I belong to *you*, body and essence and everything in between. I will never go to him without you there. When we make love again, it will be because *you* want us to, not because we want it. I need you to know this because in my mind, I would consider that…"

"Cheating," I croak out, interrupting him, squeezing his hands so tightly, they go white.

"Yes," he says, with a small smile, glad that I've got it in one guess.

I let out the breath I was holding in relief. "Thank you for saying this. I was worried. I mean, I am so glad that you were together in that way before, and not just because it was so fucking hot, but because it meant so much to you. I want you to do it again. I need you to, but I don't think I could handle it if you excluded me."

"You don't ever have to worry about that, Princess. I can assure you that this is up to you entirely. How you want us, where you want us, if you want us with each other. It's no one else's call. Just yours."

I nod, tears pricking my eyes. "I love you," I murmur to him, leaning forward to kiss him. "He enjoyed it," I add with a wicked smile.

"Oh, I know he did," he says back with a smirk so arrogant; I laugh at him.

"Pretty confident of your abilities there, aren't you?"

"Definitely. I know what I'm doing."

"That you do," I say seductively, but he shakes his head at me.

"I'm saying no. Bath and food for you."

"You're too responsible," I complain.

"Someone has to be the adult around here. You lot are like a gang of randy youths."

I snort at his patronizing attitude. "I *am* a youth," I remind him.

"Hm, I forget." His eyes cloud over and he avoids my gaze.

"What?" I ask, "what did I say?"

"We are all so much older than you, Delinda. Even Pres. It is our responsibility to protect you and take care of you."

"I can protect myself, but I appreciate the sentiment," I say with an eye roll.

"I am quite serious," he says, giving me a dark look. "Don't joke about your safety and that of our child. Considering what happened the other day, we need to be extra vigilant. We must take extra precautions, which needs discussing. All of us sleeping together isn't happening again. One of us stands watch over you and the others at all times."

"Oh, don't be ridiculous!" I scoff at him. "That means that one of you will be sleeping while I am awake."

"Shifts then," he says. "This is how it is going to be, Delinda. Even more so with Trey prowling around." His face goes menacing for a second before he adjusts it.

"I am not scared of your twin," I say. "If I can kick your ass, then I can kick his."

"Who says you can kick mine?" He looks mildly insulted.

"Oh, please. I am bigger and badder than you, and I come from a long line, well, okay, a very short line, of hot-tempered women. Trust me when I say adrenaline gets you far."

He grins and I get that he was teasing me. Jerk.

"I know you can kick ass, Princess. But do this for me, please. As your husband, I just can't sit around all day leaving you to fend for yourself. It's not who I am."

I give in, because who can argue with that? "I love who you are," I clasp my hands around the back of his neck and crawl onto his lap so that he is cradling me in his arms. I love being held by him. It is astounding how much I feel for him in such a short space of time. I want to make him happy, so I give into his need to take care of me. "Fine, do whatever is necessary to keep us all safe."

His eyes flash with triumph, and something else that I can't quite place, but it is gone before I can try to figure it out.

"Now, bath and food," he says, his mood light after the seriousness from before.

"Done," I agree with a nod and sit back to watch him, feeling such love for him. The fact that he came to me about his feelings for To'Kah and their evolving relationship means the world to me. I am sure that many men, wouldn't think twice about how I would feel about them going off and doing their own thing. It makes me wonder if To'Kah and Pres have thought about it. Probably not. As far as Rex is concerned, he was ready for this. The other two have just fallen into it by circumstance. But perhaps a quiet word with each of them, at some point, will ease my worry over it. Or maybe Rex can tell them how it is going to be. It'll probably sound better coming from him.

I don't bother to hide from the shame of passing the buck on that one. The less I sound like a jealous harpy, the better in my book.

12

~PRES~

I wake up suddenly, feeling a mild sense of panic. "Where is she?" I demand as soon as I realize that Delly isn't next to me.

"In the bath," Rex says, from over by the fireplace. He and To'Kah are lounging around, looking relaxed, so I calm down. I am a nervous wreck. I feel something bad coming. I can't quite figure out how I know this, but I just know. I don't want to worry Delinda, or the other two men, though, so I put a smile on my face and push it aside. For now. I also push aside the worry, that whatever it is, has to do with Rex's surprise twin. I'm still not convinced that Delly has dropped this. As quickly as she decided she wanted him, she dropped him. "We need to talk," Rex says, indicating that I should join them.

I nod and get up, Astralling on some jeans and t-shirt.

I feel To'Kah's eyes on me as I stroll over to them and bring myself to meet his eyes. What we did was so unexpected to me, but I needed it. I wanted it so badly, I took the chance that he might beat me to death for daring to get my cock anywhere near him. Rex, I get. They know each other and have something brewing there, but he doesn't know me, and this was clearly the first time he had ever done anything like that. Well, same goes for me. I never thought I would want my dick in a man's mouth but fuck me if it didn't feel good. I meet his gaze, trying not to blush furiously, but he just smiles at me and doesn't say anything. Thank fuck. That would have been awkward.

"Delinda has agreed to let us take care of her," Rex says to mine and To'Kah's surprise.

"Oh?" I ask. "That's..."

"Indeed," Rex says, with an eye roll. "However, we are in uncertain times right now and we cannot let anything derail her plans to claim the throne, nor put herself and the baby in any danger."

I fail to point out that if she has to *kill* her uncle to get the throne, then that will put her in immense danger. He obviously knows this, and it will be met with scorn. I have the ridiculous need to meet with his approval for some reason.

"So, we sleep in shifts from now on. One of us will be watching out at all times. Got it."

"I agree," To'Kah says, stretching out and placing his hand close to Rex, not touching him, but the intention is clear.

Rex smiles at him and then pins my gaze with a slightly harder look.

"Of course," I say quickly, needing that smile aimed at me. I get it and feel relieved.

"Good. Another thing we need to discuss is very important to Delinda and to me. I don't know how the two of you feel about this, but I will not, I repeat *not*, give Delinda any reason to be worried about our changing relationships."

"I don't know what you mean?" I ask, puzzled. "Isn't she happy that we are getting closer?" My paranoia has flared up in a flame so fierce, the execution fire pit will be jealous of it.

"Yes, of course she is," Rex says, dismissively waving his hand at me, causing the flame to drop down to a burning ember. "However, after what happened with us earlier..." he looks at To'Kah and then between me and him, "...I have informed her that no matter where this goes between us, we will not engage in any sexual behavior without her. As far as I am concerned, if we went behind her back with this, it is cheating. She agrees. We will engage only when she wants us to, with her involvement. Are we clear?"

I nod eagerly. I hadn't even thought that one of them would want me on my own. Although, he is probably talking more to To'Kah than he is to me. "Yes, I also agree. Anything outside of the four us is unacceptable."

"No, not entirely," Rex says. "She is allowed to be with one of us on her own. She is the center of this. We are *hers* and she can do with us what she likes."

"Agreed," To'Kah says easily. "I had already figured this out, anyway. I know her thoughts."

"Yes, okay, big man," Rex drawls at him. "But it had to be said."

I nod. I want to ask what they think will happen between us again, but I'm worried I will sound like a fool. The other two are being very blasé about it, so I need to be as well. I will take whatever they throw at me, because Delinda wants it, that much was clear from today, but more than that. I want it. I just want to know if they want that from me.

"Don't worry, kid, your time will come," Rex says to me with a smile that makes my cock go hard.

"Uh," I stammer, and he laughs at me.

"In the meantime, join in with what you feel comfortable with," To'Kah says, his dark eyes boring into mine, letting me know that he enjoyed what we did before.

"Okay," I bleat like a fucking idiot.

Our conversation is then drawn to a close by Delinda sweeping into the room, smelling like heaven from her bath.

"You need to get rid of him," she states, walking over to us and stopping with her fists on her hips.

"What do you mean?" Rex asks warily, standing up.

"Trey. You need to get him to leave. If he isn't here, I won't be tempted to go to him and see what is between us, and vice versa."

I jump up. "You said you weren't going to," I almost accuse her.

She turns those fierce green eyes to me, and I wither slightly inside. "I meant it. But think about it. If you knew you were one of my Chosen Ones and we didn't end up together, how would you feel? Compelled to pursue me, that's how," she states, not bothering to let me answer for myself. She turns back to Rex. "Get him to leave. Today. I don't want him here."

Rex gathers her to him, in a bone-crushing hug that she returns. "You have no idea how much I needed to hear you say that," he murmurs to her.

She pulls away and gives him a soft smile which she then turns to us. "After what happened earlier, I realized that I am truly happy with how things are. I don't want to mess with it."

I grab her hand and bring it to my lips to kiss as To'Kah also leaps up and shoves Rex out of the way. "Good," he whispers to her. "Trey is a first-class asshole. He isn't a good fit here."

I look to Rex in query, but he is staring at To'Kah like he fell from the moon. There is way more to this than just a bit of sibling rivalry. I get the impression that Trey has somehow hurt Rex in the past and To'Kah knows about it.

I suddenly feel very alone, and on the outside. It hits me hard that I am the newcomer here, and I feel like my place isn't as cemented as the other two, even as Delinda's husband. If she ever decides that *I* am not a good fit for her, it will rip my heart out.

She pushes To'Kah away from her and comes to me, searching my eyes. "Don't feel that way," she says, shaking her head. "I love you; you belong here."

I catch my breath, as the other two men stare at her in confusion. "You can feel it?" I ask.

"Yes," she says. "We are connected, my love. Bonded in a way that cannot be denied."

I gulp. The same could be said for her and Trey. I don't say anything though, I just nod at her, with a smile, and pull her in for a kiss that she returns briefly. It occurs to me that I am keeping a whole hell of a lot bottled up. I need to find the balls to speak up and face her wrath like a man. Rex and To'Kah do, so I have to, as well.

Tomorrow.

"Food," she says with a smile and off we all troop to feed the center of our world. However, a quick glance at the other two men, confirms that her words have had the exact same effect on us all.

13

~TO'KAH~

We walk in a solemn silence down to the kitchen. We have, once again, missed the gathering. Dracul is going to start kicking our asses if we don't start showing our faces. I know that my contemplative silence matches the other two men. Delinda's words, while meant to be reassuring, just drove home the point that Trey has a claim on her that can't be denied. She is right. He has to go.

I catch Rex's eye. With a grim look he tilts his head to indicate that we need to talk in private.

I nod back, wondering when we are going to get the chance to do that. I put my hand on the small of Delinda's back as we push through the kitchen doors. It is bustling with staff and they all turn to look at us as we enter, their conversation and work drawing to a halt.

"The Princess requires food," Rex states, stepping up to her side and taking control of this situation as her husband. I am still a nobody, so I step back and let him order everyone around, getting them to jump to his requests. They do exactly as he asks.

They know the score. They know who he is, and they all saw him fighting off the Emperor's Guard during my attempted execution. He was impressive to say the least.

I try to push the memory away. I am here now and that is all that matters. Being a second away from death changes nothing as far as I am concerned. I am still me, still in love with Delinda and now having a child with her. This can't affect me. I won't let it.

"How do you do it?" Pres asks me, suddenly appearing by my side.

"Do what?" I reply with a frown.

"Say what you are thinking to her. I don't want to upset her."

I snort in amusement, my own plight vanishing as I look at her Beta husband with a sympathetic look. "I didn't. For a surprisingly long time, I gave her what she wanted. It's only now that I feel that I can. That she will, at the very least, have to listen to what I am saying. You are her husband. Take that role by the horns and do right by her. Giving in to her, or letting her get away with shit, isn't doing her any favors."

He gives me a bright smile. "Thanks," he says and brushes the back of his hand against mine.

I smile back, one that I know will have him thinking about his actions earlier. He was bold, very bold, and it took me aback slightly. But when I heard Delinda's approval, I knew what I had to do.

He goes bright red, as I knew he would.

"Don't you dare apologize," I say to him before he can blurt it out. "Own it."

He nods quickly, taking in what I said. He is such a baby still. He has a lot to learn. I don't mind giving him a helping hand, especially if it helps Delinda along the way.

"I liked it," he says shyly.

"So did I," I reassure him, knowing that is what he was looking for.

He nods, and that is the end of this conversation, as Rex has Delinda sorted out with a towering plate and we head back to the bedroom.

*S*he picks at it, looking slightly green.

"Just eat what you can," I say to her gently.

She nods and shoves the plate away. "I'm done."

The three of us dive on the remains, only now realizing that we are three, full-grown male Dragons, and haven't eaten ourselves in what seems like forever. Almost dying, fucking and sleeping has taken over our lives.

We need to get our shit sorted.

"It's a couple of hours until breakfast," I say. "We need to be there."

"I agree," Rex says. "Dracul isn't going to give us much more leeway over this."

Delinda nods wearily. "I need to go and see him before then. I can't leave this any longer. It is eating me alive."

We all nod at her. Her mood is affecting ours, as we all go morose suddenly.

"Have a quick nap and then go and see him," Pres says decidedly.

"Good idea," I say, giving him the approval he needed, so that he will continue to voice his thoughts. I know he is holding back on a lot of things. I can see it on his face. His face that suddenly looks very familiar as I stare at him, taking in every inch of his features. I frown at him and he frowns back at me, second guessing himself.

"Or whatever you decide," he mumbles, and I huff at him.

"No," I say to Delinda. "Pres is right." I look back at him, wondering where I have seen him before and when.

As Delinda climbs wordlessly into bed, it strikes me. I haven't ever met Pres before, but I have met someone he looks a lot alike. He bears her features to a startling degree.

His mother.

Shanti lived here, for a very long time. She was Tiamat's top sorceress, but was executed quite suddenly, days after Delinda was born.

I heard rumors as to why, but nothing official was ever said about it.

I gulp and glance back at Delinda.

I heard one of the servants gossiping to another, which subsequently got both of them executed the very next day after Shanti. Apparently, one of them had seen Shanti take Delinda's blood and cast a spell on it.

Tiamat saw it as treason and Shanti never even stood trial. She was thrown into the pit, without warning, by Delinda's overprotective father.

"What is it?" Rex whispers to me. "You look like you are going to puke."

"Nothing," I say, shaking my head. I don't know what happened. Only rumor and speculation. It will do no good to dredge this up without cause. But suddenly, it's all I can think about. "Just hungry."

"Yeah, me too," he sighs. "We will wait until breakfast. I don't want us leaving Delinda for our own selfish needs."

"Me either," I mutter, my eyes back on Pres. What did his mother want with Delinda's blood? And what spell did she cast on her? *If* that is what actually happened. Someone, apart from Remiel, must know what really happened. But there again, as the thoughts come flooding back, there was a slew of executions that week. It seems that anyone who might have known anything, is gone.

Except me.

That leaves me only one choice. A choice that I would rather not take but feel that I have to now that this is in my head.

I shudder at the prospect. It makes me feel sick with nervousness. But I have no choice now.

I must speak to Delinda's father.

14

~DELINDA~

I trudge towards Uncle D's office, hoping that he is in there at this hour. We are only an hour off breakfast, so I assume that he is around, but this place has been so quiet since To'Kah's near death, I am starting to wonder if anyone still lives here, except us. It's worth asking, in my humble opinion.

The men wanted to accompany me, but I need to do this on my own.

I knock and wait.

"Enter," he replies straight away.

I gulp. Of course he knows it's me standing here.

I push open the door and walk in, closing the door quietly, before I turn to look at him.

I stifle my gasp. He looks a mess; like he hasn't slept in a week.

"Delinda," he says, standing up and approaching me with caution.

"Uncle D," I say.

We just stand there awkwardly.

"I must apologize…" he starts.

I shake my head. "Not to me," I say, and he nods once. "I want to clear the air though. I feel like a prisoner in my bedroom. I am reluctant to come out in case something happens again."

He looks grim-faced at me. "That was completely unsanctioned," he says. "Those responsible for that witch-hunt have been dealt with. I know that I overreacted, somewhat, to the news, but you must understand that it was a shock to me. I trusted you. Both. You both deeply disappointed me."

"We know," I say, trying to hold back the tears. "We are so sorry, Uncle D. It was selfish, and we didn't think of the consequences. We fell in love a long time ago and acted upon it. It was wrong, but it doesn't change the facts now."

"Hmm," he says with a massive sigh. "How are you feeling?"

I shrug. "I'm okay, all of this notwithstanding."

"Indeed," he mutters. "And the men?"

"They're okay too. Worried about what is going on around here." I blame them for my next question. "Are we alone now? Just the family?"

"No, but everyone has been told to stay out of your way."

"Oh."

Awkward silence.

"You need to talk to To'Kah," I blurt out.

"I will."

"You go to him. He deserves that much," I point out forcefully.

"I will," he replies, infuriatingly calm. Then he gives me a desperate look. "Is he doing okay?"

"Considering he was seconds away from being burned alive, he is doing remarkably well," I say, with such a ferocious glare at my uncle, he looks away.

"Yes, well. Did you thank your father properly for saving him?" he asks, looking back at me, with a look that signifies he is done feeling bad about it and now he is back to business.

"I will," I say, giving him the same bland response, he did to me.

He stifles his snort as he acknowledges it.

"I need to know how the transfer of Power happens, you know, when I take the throne." I change the subject to catch him off-guard.

He doesn't look surprised by my question. "You've heard how I got the Power?"

"Yes," I say. "I know it transferred to you because you killed Grandmother. Does this mean I have to kill you?"

He snickers at me. Well, it would be a snicker, if he was anything less that the Dragon Emperor.

"No," he says. "The Power is yours, Delinda. It transferred to me because I killed Tiamat and was the only Dragon in the vicinity that it could pass to. Well, the only *real* one," he adds derisively. "You have to earn it, of course, be deemed worthy of it, but the ceremony to give it to you is less bloody than that."

Why don't I believe him? What he says makes sense, but he is looking a bit shifty and it doesn't inspire confidence in his words.

"Okay," I say, brightly, hoping that I am wrong and that it is all going to be easy-peasey. "I'm guessing there are trials and tests?"

"No," he says. "The Power will decide if it wants you to take it or stay with me. This is why you need to be ready, Delinda. I cannot stress this to you enough. One hundred percent commitment to this for the *right* reasons." His green eyes pin mine and I gulp. Oh, he knows me too well.

"I *do* want it for the right reasons," I say, and he raises his eyebrow at me. "Sure, I want the perks that come with it," I add to his amusement. "But this is my destiny and I am ready to take it. I will do whatever it takes."

He nods slowly. "I know you know that Rexus's twin is here, and what he is. I am giving you one chance, right now, to decide his fate."

I frown at him. What? Now, that makes no sense. Is he saying he will let me take him if I want him? I was so sure he would be dead set against it, especially after what Rex said. I waver in my promise to my men. I gave in to them because it was what they wanted, and I didn't want anything to happen to Trey. I was going to reject him and send him packing. Now? If I can have a chance with him, what do I do? Will my men ever accept him, or will it cause a rift that won't be fixed?

"I…" I start and then just look at him.

"One chance," he states.

I blink.

Time passes as I remain silent

"I…send him away," I croak out.

He nods once. "Good choice," he says.

I get the very real feeling that it was a test. Regardless of what he said about no trials, I think he is lying.

"See you at breakfast," I choke. I make it to the door and then a thought occurs to me, so I turn back to him. "And make sure that there is a seat for To'Kah."

His jaw goes tight, and he grits out, "Of course," before he goes back to his desk and I leave, needing to get back to my men.

15

~REX~

"I am going to speak to Trey," I say to To'Kah. "Tell him what Delinda has said and tell him to go."

"Leave it to Dracul," he says earnestly. "The less you have to deal with him, the better."

"Yeah, but *I* want to be the one that tells him she doesn't want him. See his asshole face fall," I say vehemently.

"Okay, I get that. But I am going to see Dracul now and tell him as well. As soon as he knows Delinda wants him gone, he will be," To'Kah says.

I pause. "You don't have to do that. You *shouldn't*."

"I'm okay," he insists. "And this needs dealing with first and foremost. My issue is second to Delinda's happiness and well-being."

"So…there *is* an issue?" I press.

He huffs at me in exasperation. "No. There isn't. Go now so that you are back when Delinda returns. I will intercept Dracul and tell him of her wishes."

"Fine," I say, but I am dubious. He shouldn't be going to see the man who tried to kill him, on his own, so soon. "But take Pres with you," I add firmly.

"No!" he snaps at me. "I am a grown-ass Dragon, I can take care of this alone." He storms off in a proper pissy mood, so I leave it and head towards my old room. I kick it open, to find Trey standing back, as if he knew I was already coming.

"You are leaving, and that is final," I state, lounging in the doorway, trying to play it cool, facing off with my hated twin.

"Not if she doesn't want me too," Trey replies.

"She does. She informed me to do whatever it takes to get rid of you. Don't think for a second that I won't do exactly that," I threaten him.

"Still so sore after all these years," he drawls at me. "Share and share alike, Brother."

"Never," I spit at him, standing up straight and clenching my fists in an effort not to punch his lights out. "You will never get your talons into my wife, are we clear?"

"I did it before," he goads me. "I am sure I can do it again, especially as this wife is supposed to be with me."

I breathe in deeply and push that aside. It will do no one any good to be seen grappling in the hallway with my evil twin. "She is mine. We are bonded. You are just…" I wave my hand around dismissively, "…my clone. That is all. You have no real connection to her."

"That's not what she thinks. She knew what hit her when I touched her, and so do I."

His brown eyes go slightly darker as he says this. I know he is thinking about my wife in the way that *I* think about her: naked and on top of me, fucking me until I want to weep with the joy of it. "I will never let you take what is mine again. Are we clear?" I say, quietly so that he knows I am being deadly serious.

"But she wants it," he insists.

"Nope, she wants you gone. She is happy with me; she doesn't want a weaker version."

"Oh, please. She is probably dripping with the thought of taking twins. They always are," he snorts.

That's it! I draw my fist back and punch him square in the face. "How dare you disrespect my wife," I spit at him, kicking his ankles out from under him and then issuing another kick to his ribs when he falls. "You know I can beat you, so don't even think about getting up," I add when he tries to get to his knees.

He pants at me with an evil grin on his face. "Maybe before. I've had an upgrade," he rasps.

I watch him warily as he gets to his feet and flicks out his hand to send me sprawling across the wide hallway. What the fuck? He has never had that kind of magick before.

"I am giving you a choice," he says, striding towards me. "We either do this together, or I am going to get rid of you and take your place."

I get to my feet and smirk at him. "If you kill me and try to take my place, you will be waiting for a particularly long time. She will be devastated and blame you. You will never get her that way."

"Who said anything about killing you?" he asks, returning the smirk. "I am talking about getting you out of the way and *becoming* you."

It takes me a moment, but it hits me, and I burst out laughing. "Oh, you have got to be joking. She knows me. She will never think that you are me."

"I'm willing to take that chance. Besides, if there is no one to refute it, then…"

He leaves that sentence dangling and I gulp. Is he right? We look exactly the same. Would Delinda know the difference if he went to her as me? I hope that she would, but the doubt lurks. We barely know each other. Does she know enough about me to spot a fake?

I can't let that happen.

I attack, but he knows I am coming and sends that magick my way again. It hits me in the chest, and I grunt in pain, struggling to breathe.

I look down, the blood gurgling in my mouth and spilling out. I have a huge hole in my chest where that bolt of Black magick hit me. I know what it is. I can feel the evil working its way through me. I always knew Trey was a nasty son-of-a-bitch, but to mess with this kind of shit…he is in way over his head. I drop to my knees, willing myself to get back up and get to Delinda but another blow from Trey sends me down, crashing to the stone floor. My eyes close of their own accord and the blackness envelopes me.

16

~DELINDA~

I'm greeted outside the room by Rex. He is looking a bit flustered, and he is staggering like he was hit by Dracul in full flight.

"Everything okay?" I ask immediately, taking his hand.

He grips it tightly, staring at our joined hands.

"Yes," he breathes. "I can't get used to that," he adds, looking back up at me with a wide grin.

I give him one back. He seems so much more relaxed today. I guess it has all been quite tense since we got married, what with one thing and another. I'm glad that he feels that he can relax a bit now.

"Me either," I tell him. "I love feeling this with you and Pres."

"Mm," he murmurs. "I need to talk to you about something."

"Okay," I say and let him Astral me off.

We land in his old bedroom. He draws me into a kiss, pressing his lips to mine and slipping his tongue in my mouth. He groans and deepens it, as I cling to him. His hands skim over my breasts and around to my ass, which he squeezes hard.

"Later," I say, pushing him away. "We don't have much time."

"Fine. I'll get straight to the point, Delinda," he says. "I've had a change of heart. About Trey."

I frown at him. "What do you mean?"

"I think you should pursue the connection that you have with him. It is not fair to you to deny it."

"Is this because of what I said to Pres?" I ask, this suddenly making sense. "I didn't mean it about Trey. I don't know him, and you were quite specific about your feelings on it." I am so confused right now; my head is spinning. Did I make the wrong choice with Uncle D?

"Indeed," he growls at me, suddenly looking pissed off, but then his face relaxes again. "I have thought about how this affects *you*, Delinda. My feelings shouldn't count in this."

"What?" I exclaim. "You can't be serious?"

"Oh, I am," he says, squeezing my hand.

"Oh, wow," I murmur. "I—I decided to leave it. I don't understand why you want me to give him a chance. Besides, To'Kah and Pres will need to agree to this, and I don't see them having the same thoughts as you about it."

"I will talk to them, make them see that this is about you, Delinda, not us," he says with a shrug, appearing so unconcerned, it makes me hope that this is true and not another test from my Uncle.

"Delinda?" he presses me.

I blink at him. He has used my name more times in this conversation than he has over the last three days. He usually calls me 'Princess', or 'Little Dragon'.

"Uhm, I guess I will have to think about it, based on what the other men say," I decide. This is just too weird.

"No," he snaps at me. "Their opinion doesn't matter. He is *my* brother and I am telling you that you can bring him in."

"Rex," I start, getting pissed off with this now. "I said I would think about it." Even if I have already decided that I will pursue Trey, Rex's attitude is getting on my nerves. "It's time to go to breakfast now. We need to find Pres and To'Kah."

"Okay," he says, visibly backing down, which is also odd. "I'm sorry, Delinda. I just wanted you to know that it's okay as far as I am concerned."

I smile tightly at him and Astral us back upstairs, where To'Kah is waiting for us.

"Everything okay?" To'Kah asks immediately, giving Rex a hard look before he turns to me.

"Yes, fine," I start to say as Rex interrupts me with, "I've told Delinda she can pursue things with Trey."

"What?" To'Kah snaps, his eyes boring into Rex's and then narrowing into two vicious slits. "Delinda, get away from him now."

I look between the two of them in confusion. "What is going on?"

"That isn't Rex," To'Kah grits out jabbing his finger at Rex.

"What?" I ask, stepping closer to To'Kah.

"Don't be ridiculous," Rex scoffs at him.

"Delly!" Pres cries, racing into the room and diverting the attention to himself. "You need to come quickly!"

"What is it?" I demand, the blood draining from my face at his urgency.

"Trey has been imprisoned and Dracul is ready to fire him into the pit, but he's claiming he isn't Trey. He says he's Rex."

"WHAT?" I thunder, spinning back to Trey. He is looking back at me in shock.

"I knew it," To'Kah hisses at him.

"Whoa, wait," Rex, or Trey, or whoever, says, putting his hands up. "I'm Rex."

I search his face. He *looks* like Rex. But he isn't acting like my husband.

I turn from him and grab To'Kah's hand. "Don't let him get away!" I spit back at Trey, knowing it has to be him now. Then I let him go and grab Pres. "Take me to him."

Pres nods and Astrals us off.

73

17

~PRES~

We land as close to the fire pit as I dare to go with Delinda being pregnant. I can't risk the crowd going wild and her accidentally ending up in it.

"What is this about?" she cries at her uncle, stalking over to him anyway.

"Is this your husband?" he demands her.

She looks at Trey chained up on his knees at Dracul's feet, looking a little beaten and fried, by something evil, but alive and kicking.

I see her falter. She has no idea. Neither do I. They look exactly the same. "Ask him something," I whisper to her.

He gives me a withering gaze, and it confirms it for me. That's Rex. But how do we convince the Emperor? He is hell-bent on executing some poor fucker this week, that's for sure.

"What did we talk about in the bathroom earlier on?" she asks straight away.

"What defines cheating in our relationship," he growls at her.

"That's Rex," she says quickly, shooting him an apologetic look.

"I'm afraid, I can't take that as proof," Dracul says. "We

found these in your room." He throws something at her, and she gasps.

I look down at her hands and gulp. "Someone has been spying on us?" I blurt out and then cringe as Dracul's eyes land on me.

"Anything he says, could have been gleaned from these orbs," Dracul says.

"You bastard!" Delinda shrieks, dropping the orbs and stamping on them furiously. "How dare you!" She goes for Rex, uhm Trey, with her talons drawn.

Fuck's sake. I'm getting really confused.

"Princess," Rex snarls at her, ducking out of the way of her talons. "Look at me. You know me."

She stops. She looks between me and him. I can see the recognition in her eyes. She knows without doubt.

"I see," he says, looking down. "You have no idea, do you?"

She opens her mouth to say something but gets interrupted.

"That is Trey!" Rex says from behind us, struggling with To'Kah, who, to his credit, isn't running away from the fire pit, like I would be had I been in his shoes.

"No!" To'Kah roars, grabbing him by his collar. "This is Trey."

"ENOUGH!" Dracul bellows and everyone goes silent. "Delinda?"

"Let me cast a spell," I say quickly, letting her off the hook.

"What kind?" Dracul asks.

I breathe out in relief that he is taking me seriously. "A trace. It's…" I look between Delinda and To'Kah, "Rex has been with both of you, I can trace the scent," I whisper so quietly, even Dracul didn't hear me.

"Speak up!" he commands me.

"Do it!" Delinda practically shrieks at me, looking back at the man kneeling before Dracul. "I know it's you," she says to him before she glares over at the other one. "*He* keeps calling me Delinda."

Rex smirks at her. "Oh, Little Dragon. You have made me fall in love with you all over again," he says.

She grins at him.

I must act quickly now. The crowds are baying for blood after they were riled up and denied a few days ago. To'Kah drags Trey closer to Delinda.

I turn to Dracul, ready to explain what I am going to do when a 'whoosh' behind him makes me stop, mouth open.

Dracul's eyes narrow and he turns, annoyed.

"Septimus," he drawls.

The Dragon Prince glares at the Emperor with something close to loathing. His blonde hair is long, longer than To'Kah's, flowing down his back, his green eyes sharp and like ice. I hear a gasp behind me and turn slightly to see Aefre and Remiel have shown up. Delinda's mother is staring at the newcomer in utter disbelief, her mouth hanging open.

"I allowed my son to reside here instead of at home because I knew you would watch over him," he hisses. "Now, I see you are about to execute him!" He advances, talons drawn, but Dracul stops him with a hand up and a flash of magick.

Septimus growls at him.

I look at Delinda and she looks back at me. We are both completely in the dark here.

"Dad," Rex whines, still kneeling on the ground. "What the fuck. Go away. I can fight my own battles."

"Dad?" Delinda mouths at him.

He rolls his eyes skyward and then clambers to his feet awkwardly with his hands chained behind his back.

"Clearly not," Septimus snarls at him, hauling him the rest of the way to his feet by his elbow. "Dracul, you have some explaining to do."

"Short version. We thought he was Trey'Za," Dracul says, not beating around the bush.

I gulp when Septimus turns to his younger twin son and pins him with a vicious stare. "Up to no good again?" he asks nastily.

"Wait! Just wait a damn minute here!" Delinda shrieks. "What the fuck is going on?"

"Delinda!" Remiel snaps at her. "Language."

"Princess," Rex says resigned. "Meet my father, Septimus, Dragon Prince and also your Uncle."

I gulp. "What?" I blurt out. "That makes you cousins!" I feel sick to my stomach. What the fuck is going on indeed?

"Hardly," Rex drawls. "Her heritage is such a cluster fuck…"

"Hey," Delinda snaps at him at the same time as Aefre.

"Someone is going to have to explain it to me," I say, feeling a bit faint.

"I will," To'Kah says, grabbing me by the arm. He bends to kiss Delinda chastely on the forehead. "Deal with your family drama, and we will see you soon."

She nods dumbly at him.

I watch as Septimus bows to her and she glares down her nose at him, offering her hand to him. He smirks at her and takes it, kissing her knuckles. The last thing I see, before To'Kah Astrals me away in disgust, is Aefre choking back a retch as Delinda stumbles back from the force of the Chosen bond.

18

~TO'KAH~

"No!" Pres roars as we land back in the bedroom.

I shake him as he is about to Astral back outside. "Stay out of it," I warn him. "Trust me, we are better off up here, out of the way. Things are about to get ugly."

"Start at the beginning," he growls at me. "What the fuck is going on?"

"Tiamat was Dracul and Septimus's mother. She was also Aefre's mother, but not by birth. Only by essence, and a loophole in a curse, was she born to Tiamat. Her parents, her *human* parents, were Anglo-Saxon peasants in the year 996."

He gapes at me.

"The birthright and Power were passed down to her, but with all curses, there were complications. She needed to be strong enough to bear the Power. Constantine Aquila, one of her current husbands, was sent to her to turn her on holy ground, so that the Vampire she became could ignite the Dragon power inside her. It didn't happen and a long story short, it was only back in 2012, that she managed to get herself into a holy union with a Chosen One. But not really a Dragon Chosen one, just another one of Laurentis's sons, in Remiel's absence."

"Fuck. My head hurts," Pres moans, sitting down.

"Like we said, it's a cluster fuck."

"So Delly and Rex aren't really related by blood as such, just Power?"

"Precisely."

"You saw what I did, didn't you?"

"I did."

"How is this happening?" he asks me.

I shrug. "Who knows? What I do know, is that Septimus probably won't just walk away."

"But Dracul was going to kill Trey to stop him from messing with Delly. Is he going to kill his own brother now as well?"

"Guess we will have to wait and see." I slump down next to him.

"So, Trey took Rex's place to convince Delly to give him a chance?"

"Seems that way."

"How did this get so complicated?" he asks me, close to tears.

The door bursts open before I can hand out some platitude and Delinda sweeps in with Rex hot on her heels. "Not a fucking chance, Delinda."

"Oh, you don't have to convince me!" she shouts at him. "I was okay with bringing Trey in, before I got a taste of what an asshole he is, but your father? Nuh-Uh."

Pres and I jump up. "What is happening?" I ask.

"Delly," Pres says imploringly.

"Don't worry," she says, turning to us with a soft smile. "Trey was booted out of the Realm by his father, then Septimus staked a claim on me as a Chosen One, making Uncle D turn green and firmly forbidding it."

"So did Aefre and Remiel," Rex adds. "He is a filthy pervert if he thinks he is getting his hands on you. He is over four thousand years old! This is…"

He looks utterly defeated.

"Why did you never tell me who your father is?" Delinda asks him.

"Why? What does it matter?"

"You are a Prince. A royal."

"No, I'm not." He taps his back to indicate the lack of a Dragon marking, which only the royals bear.

"How did that happen?" she asks.

"My mother was a commoner, a servant, very low on the totem pole. It was never in the cards."

"Jesus," she mutters. "I can't get my head around this. He thinks he is the original Chosen one and that you two inherited it from him. He isn't going to drop this." Her panic is evident.

"We will deal with it," I tell her, giving her a hug that I needed from her. I can't think about her slipping through my fingers now that I've got her. It's too much after everything else that's happened.

"Delly!" Aefre exclaims, bursting through the door without even bothering to knock. "We need to talk."

"Yeah," she says, pulling away from me.

"Alone!" Aefre barks at us.

"It's okay. Go. I'll catch up with you later," Delinda says with a weak smile.

There is nothing left but for the three of us to troop out, looking lost. But as I walk past Aefre, she grabs my arm, her cold hand gripping me tightly. I freeze, and so does Delinda, her eyes going straight to where Aefre is touching me. It is the first time we have touched since the last time I saw to her as her Guardian. I won't deny that my Dragon lights up at the contact with His former charge, but all I want is to run away and hide from Delinda's vicious snarl. *She* is not amused.

However, when I look up into Aefre's green eyes, exactly the same as her daughter's, all I see is a cold glare and feel the ice in the air. Her Fae powers have kicked in and it repulses me. Like all Dragons, we loathe the Fae. She was only accepted because of who she is, who her mother was. It has been overlooked that her father is King of the Dark Fae, as she favored her Dragon Powers over her Fae ones. It is blindingly apparent now that she has full control of her Fae Powers and if I had any lingering feelings of any kind for her, I don't now. I am so glad that Delinda never inherited any Fae powers from her mother. It might have changed the course of our relationship if she had shown signs of them.

"Make no mistake that you are here for one reason only," she hisses at me. "Her father saved you so that our grandchild can have a father. Their real father. But let me make this very clear to you. If that child comes out and looks like one of them," she indicates her head at Rex and Pres, who had paused in the doorway when Aefre grabbed me, "Remiel will shove you into that pit so fast, you won't know what hit you."

"Understood," I growl at her and try to shake her hand off my arm.

She lets go, only because she wanted to, not out of my strength, and the warmth hits me again. I think she was trying to freeze me from the inside out.

I push past her as Delinda snarls at her mother, but I bang the door closed and take a deep breath. I avoid looking at Rex and Pres for a moment, knowing that their faces will reflect the fear that I know is on mine. I know without a doubt that she means it. If that child isn't mine, I am a goner. For good this time. But that fear doesn't stop what I need to do. There is no getting away from the fact that I need to go to Remiel, to thank him for saving me regardless of why he did it, and to find out what the fuck went down with Pres's mother.

"I'll catch up with you later," I mutter to the two men and Astral off before they can say anything.

19

~DELINDA~

"Don't threaten him again!" I shriek at her, but she puts her hand up to stop me.

"We can discuss that, at length, another time," she snaps at me. "You are in some big trouble here, missy!" Her low growl stops my tirade and I quiver as her words, and the last few minutes, sink in.

"What am I going to do?" I cry, falling into her arms, needing her to tell me. I am in way over my head here.

She holds me tightly, consoling me for a minute before she gently pushes me away to look up at me.

"At least Trey'Za is gone," she states, getting down to business. "But this new development is…not good."

"Gee, way to sugar coat it," I bark at her. "I know that I am up shit creek. The Dragon Prince, and your brother, no less." I shudder in disgust.

"*A* Dragon Prince," she points out as if that makes any fucking difference. "And the relations thing really isn't an issue. You know how complicated it is. Christ, I wouldn't be with your father if it weren't."

I gulp and feel nauseous. I forgot about that. I think Papa was Tiamat's grandnephew. The gods only know what that makes him to mother, *if* the relations thing was an issue. My head hurts trying to work it out, but I push it aside as I have got my own shit to deal with right now.

"How has this happened?" I ask her desperately.

"I don't know," she says honestly with a sigh. "I didn't even know that Septimus was still alive. And your uncle sure kept it quiet that he was Rexus's father."

"You knew about him?"

"Yeah, he was also responsible for creating the Demon race, not just Dracul. They have a House named after him and they tried to claim me once, before I married Xane…" She waves her hand around. "All beside the point. What we have to do *now* is come up with a way to sever that bond."

"How?" I shriek, my nerves taking me over again. "And won't that also sever the bond with Rex?"

"Yes, it will. But do you really want to shack up with his father as well? Who happens to be over four thousand years old! Filthy fucking pervert!" She loses it for a moment, before she takes a deep breath and gets herself back under control.

"Do you think he knew? That's why he came here?" I ask quietly. "I mean that's why Trey came."

"Of course," she snorts. "You are the True Heir, Delly. Everyone wants a piece of you."

"I don't want this," I say, suddenly exhausted. "I just want to go back to the way things were a week ago."

"Then you wouldn't have your husbands," she says, sitting me down on the bed and joining me, gripping my hand tightly.

"Don't suppose the connection is inherited from your side?" I ask hopefully. "You touch him, see if he is actually yours."

"Jesus, don't let your father hear you say that," she chuckles. "And don't get me started on CK."

"I'm serious," I snap at her.

"I doubt it. Besides, then Rexus would also be mine. Is that what you want?"

"No!" I yell and then throw up on the floor, not even caring about the mess I've just made.

Mother doesn't make a fuss though, she just waves her hand, and it's gone. To where, I don't want to know, and I don't ask.

"Come." She leads me to the bathroom and sits me on the side of the bath, aimed towards the toilet. "You have had too much stress for that little baby," she says kindly.

"I know," I weep into a washcloth that I picked up from the side of the bath. "Help me," I add with a whisper.

"I will, you don't have to worry about that," she replies stroking my back. "Delly…"

"What?" I ask after a beat.

"Were you aware that your Fae powers are showing themselves?"

I look up at her. She looks very concerned about this.

"No, I didn't. How?"

"When you get very stressed or angry, a white and gold glow appears." She waves her hand around my head. "Do your men know about your real father?" Her eyes bore into mine. "To'Kah was around at that time," she adds gently. "He knew what happened to me. Has he ever mentioned to you that he knows?"

"No," I say, shaking my head. "I thought it was a secret?" I frown at her.

"It is. You cannot tell them. The Dragons hate the Fae, Delly. You must keep up the pretense that Remiel is your real father. It could severely affect your authority here if they know."

"So, who knows then, just Uncle D? What about Septimus?"

She shrugs. "As far as I know, just Dracul."

"What has this got to do with anything?" I ask.

"Just an observation that needs to be kept in check."

"Okay," I nod. "I won't tell them. Unless the child also starts to have Fae powers. Then I will have to."

84

"Hopefully not. Your men are all pure-blood Dragons. It should be enough to squash any Fae power." She bites her lip.

"What?" I ask again.

"Nothing," she says, but there is definitely something on her mind.

Then it hits me. "I know you are hoping that To'Kah isn't the father. But he is," I say forcefully.

She just nods her head slowly. "So, about Septimus, we need to find a way to sever this connection. Yes, you will lose Rexus as well, but it is for the best."

"This whole Chosen thing has been made a complete mockery of!" I exclaim. "I wish that I had never known about it."

"I know," she sighs, and strokes my back. "But it really is an anomaly. You are supposed to have only one."

"You didn't," I accuse her. "You had, *have*, several of your own."

"Hm, not really. Your father was always the one."

"But CK, Devon and Cole were all Chosen as well because Papa was dead." I have to make her see that I am not the only freak here. She is as well. I need the company.

She looks up at me and blinks.

"What?" I ask again. "And don't tell me nothing."

"Erm," she says. "Maybe keeping the Fae thing under wraps isn't the way to go now. Maybe outing yourself as a Light Fae Princess, and their blessed baby, no less, will bring forth an outcome that will remove Septimus from your life."

"How?" I spit at her.

"It will allow your Fae mate access to you."

"No!" I say standing up and pushing aside the dizzy spell that consumes me. "Absolutely not. I am a Dragon. First and foremost. My men will not accept it. Or is that part of your plan? To have them all reject me?"

"Don't be silly," she says lightly. "I am trying to think of a way to fix this mess."

"Well, that isn't it," I say firmly, sitting back down and

sinking my swimming head into my hands. "And who is my Fae mate, anyway?" I can't help it.

"Who knows? It was just a thought."

"Look, I appreciate the help, but I am not going that way. We need to find another way."

"I will speak to your father. If anyone will protect you from Septimus, it's him. He probably already has an idea to throw him into the fire pit."

I look up at her in hope, but she was joking.

"You are no help," I whine.

"I'm sorry, love. I admit that I am at a bit of a loss with this one."

"As far as I can see, there is only one way. Claim the throne now and then no one can touch me."

"I fear you may be right," she agrees with me. "Are you ready to do this? Today?"

"No," I answer with a tremor in my voice. "Get me Uncle D, will you? I need to talk to him about this."

"Of course," she says and Astrals off leaving me alone and in fear of my future.

20

~PRES~

"What do you think they are talking about?" I ask Rex. We are sitting in one of the communal areas, staring at the doorway as if we expect Delinda to sweep in and tell us everything is going to be okay.

He shrugs. "Who knows? But if Aefre is trying to persuade her to accept my father as her Chosen One, I will kill her myself and face Remiel's wrath like a man."

I snort, but it's so *not* funny.

"Could you really have done that trace spell?" he asks me suddenly.

"Yeah, my mother taught me. I'd have had to tweak it, of course."

"And you can do that? Improvise?"

"Sure, it's easy if you know what you are doing."

He gives me a contemplative look. "Can you cast a spell on Delinda to sever the Chosen bond?"

I freeze. "What?" I splutter after a moment.

"You heard me," he says quietly, sitting forward. "Can you do it?"

"I don't know," I say, starting to panic. If this is the only way, where will that leave me and Delinda?

"Look," he says, putting his hand on my knee.

I stare at it. It is the first time he has touched me in this way.

"If you can sever the Chosen bond but *create* a new bond between just the four of us, one that will exclude everyone else and that no one else can ever be a part of, it will secure our future with her."

I look back up at him. "I can try," I start.

"No, you have to know if you can do this," Rex says urgently.

"There is a spell that will tie our lives together," I whisper to him. "It's part Blood magick, mostly Black magick, very dangerous. Delinda would have to be the anchor as the most powerful one of us and our lives would be tied to her. It would also save To'Kah in the event that…you know…"

Rex is staring at me as if I just handed him a chest of gold. "Are you serious?"

"Very," I say.

"But what about the severing? Can you do that?"

"The only way I know of that a connection can be severed is by death. I am not killing her!"

"I am not asking you to, idiot," he hisses at me. "But, is there a way to make the connection *think* it?"

"Meaning?" I ask warily.

"On Earth, there is this mix of drugs that stops your heart. You die but inject another drug and your heart starts beating again. Can you do a magic version of that?"

I blink rapidly. I have never been to Earth. I have no understanding what the fuck he is talking about. Why would a human want to do that in the first place?

"Can you?" he urges.

I want to say yes, but I have no idea if I can do this. "We need to talk to Delinda about this," I state, trying to deflect. "And To'Kah."

"Can you do it?" he enunciates.

"Yes," I say, because I need him to approve of me. It's stupid and needy but it is what it is.

He sits back relaxed and sighs. "Make the preparations. The sooner we do this, the better."

I nod and sit back too until he glares at me to get moving.

I leap up and head towards the room that Dracul showed me the day after I married Delinda. It was my mother's work room. All of her spell books, ingredients and equipment are still in there, right where she left them. All except for one cupboard that has been stripped bare. The lock was torn from it and the talon marks on the shelves indicates someone was in a rage when they dragged everything out of it. I wonder, not for the first time, what was in there, but I have work to do now.

I look down the row of spell books and find the two that I need to *create* the link, but not the one to sever a link. Or at least, I have no idea what I am looking for. It could be right in front of my nose and I wouldn't know about it.

"Think, think," I mutter to myself, but it is useless. *I* am useless. I can't even do this to save our marriage. I am letting us all down.

I sink onto a stool and put my forehead on the workbench.

"Need some help?" A voice asks me from above my head.

I look up and see Aefre looking down at me.

"I—I, erm…"

"I assume you are in here trying to find a way to sever the Chosen connection," she says astutely, looking around.

"I—I…"

I am completely speechless. It is the only time I have been alone with her, well except for the quick Astral she did with me, in and out of Delinda's room the night before the wedding. She is the Queen, she is Delly's mother, and she is something else altogether. I gulp, unable to help staring at her. Delinda looks so much like her, it's freaky. But this woman is slight, whereas Delinda has curves that make my mouth water.

"It's okay," she says, looking back at me. "Dracul told me where to find you."

"He knows I'm in here?" I croak.

"You Astralled here," she points out and I cringe.

Way to be stealthy, asshole.

She laughs at me. "It's okay, he is actually on board with this plan in ways you can't even imagine."

"If he thinks that it will destroy our marriage and then he can get her to pick just one, he is mistaken!" I say, standing up and facing off with her. I tower over her but the look she gives me makes me feel two inches tall.

"Get over that paranoia. It won't help Delinda," she snaps at me. "In case you hadn't noticed she is in deep shit here."

"I had," I mutter, feeling like a fool. "I know what I have to do, but I am unsure how to do it. The first part anyway."

She narrows her eyes at me. "What is the second part?"

"There's this ritual. It's part Blood magick, part Black…"

"I know it. I have it with my husbands," she says briskly, putting her hands on her hips.

"You do?" I ask intently. This is great news. I can use all the help I can get.

"Yes, CK performed it. He is my…erm…my, uhm." She waves her hand as if that explains who CK is. I haven't got a clue. A husband, obviously, but what else is a mystery.

"Can you get him here?" I ask her.

"Sadly, no. But I am sure I can help you with it."

She looks fully confident of her words, but I am not so sure.

"Okay, but that's secondary. I need to figure out the severing spell first."

"Yes, that is going to be tricky. A Chosen connection can only be severed with death."

"I know," I say to her with a smile.

She blinks at me and returns it. "So, where do we start with that?"

"Rex mentioned something about cheating death on Earth. I suppose I can create something that will effectively kill Delinda and bring her back."

"You are going to have to be one hundred percent sure. That's my daughter and grandchild you are talking about."

"And my wife," I point out. "Any ideas?"

She puts her hand on my arm and it lingers there as I stare at it. It feels way too nice there. Like it is supposed to be there.

She gives me an interested look but dismisses it and removes her hand.

I clap my hand back onto hers. "What is that?" I ask her.

She shrugs.

"I didn't feel that the night you took me to Delinda. What is that? Why do I feel it now?" I press. Something isn't right here.

"I am starting to think there is a lot more here than meets the eye," she mutters at me. "Your mother was a powerful witch, wasn't she?"

"What of it?" I growl at her. What is she implying?

"Word is, she was executed the day after Delinda was born for taking her blood and casting a spell on it. She made sure you were going to be Chosen when the time was right, didn't she? Trouble is, her blood is of my blood." Her penetrating look makes me feel sick to my stomach.

"My mother wouldn't do that," I choke out. Or would she? She always told me that I was destined for great things. That the Princess would be mine and that our family legacy would live on through our children. I didn't believe her, obviously, I thought she was just being a mother and saying the things she hoped would happen for her child.

But when I was summoned here the night before I met Delinda, my father explained the Chosen bond to me. Told me what to look out for if I was lucky enough to touch the Princess.

Fuuuuuuck.

I gulp, my head swimming. I sit back on the stool, still staring into those green eyes.

"Thought so," she says with a nod. "You didn't know about it though, did you?"

I shake my head at her. I am dead, DEAD, if Dracul finds out about this. As it sinks in, it feels like my heart has been ripped out. I am not really Delinda's destiny. My mother ensured it and died for it, just so that I could marry the Princess and secure the family legacy.

"It doesn't matter anyway," Aefre says softly, taking my hand. "If you sever the connection, it will be gone anyway, and you are going to create a new bond between the three of you."

"Four of us," I rasp.

Her face turns to one of disgust. "Oh, yes, *four*."

"Why do you hate him so much?" I blurt out.

"It goes back to a long time ago," she says.

"You need to get over it," I say to her, as she did to me. "He is a part of Delinda's life now."

"He abandoned me!" she spits out, with so much venom, I flinch. "And then he took my daughter from me. I know he is the reason she didn't want to come home!"

She bangs her fist on the table and then visibly calms herself.

"Oh," I say, because there is nothing else I can say or do that will change how she feels.

She puts her hand back on my arm and I jump. "If that isn't enough to get your arse moving on a solution to this, then nothing will be."

Well, she is not wrong. No way can I be bound to her as well.

Shit. Fuck. What has my mother done?

I nod quickly and look around. "It is going to take me several days to go through all of this."

Aefre looks around as well. "I may know of a quicker way. Meet me back here in an hour." She Astrals off and I breathe a sigh of relief. It was getting way too small in here with her standing there looking at me with those pretty green eyes. I will bring Rex with me when I come back. Or better yet, To'Kah. At least I know then she will be all glares and grimaces, not soft looks and smiles. For now, I need to find Delinda and seek reassurance from her that everything is going to be okay. I Astral back to her, only to be slammed out of the room by such a force, it makes me bounce back through space to the work room.

"Fuck!" I roar, rubbing my aching head. "What the fuck was that?"

21

~REX~

I tap my fingers impatiently. Where the fuck are Delinda and To'Kah? I sent Pres away about half an hour ago, but he has work to do, so I don't expect to see him anytime soon.

That is until he rushes towards me, face fraught and looking like he has Astralled into a solid concrete wall.

"What is it?" I ask standing up. "Did you find something?"

"Yeah, I'll get to that in a bit. You need to come now."

He races towards the stairs on foot, so I follow him, a feeling of panic rising up. "What's happened?"

"I dunno. I tried to Astral into our room, but I got flung back, all the way back to the work room," he pants at me, taking the stairs two at a time.

"If that's my father, I will kill him!" I roar and rush past Pres to smash into the bedroom door.

It shakes under the force, but the magick stay in place, quivering visibly it is so strong.

I bang on it with my fist and I hear Delinda shout, "We're okay! Leave us!"

"Fat chance, Princess!" I yell back. "Is my father in there

with you? I swear to the gods, I will kill him if he has touched you."

"Oh, calm down," Dracul says, opening the door and dropping the barrier so that I fall into the room in a most undignified manner. "The things I have to say to Delinda are private. Please go away."

It's not a request.

I back out, with my hands up, but on my way out, I say, "Please don't let him anywhere near her."

"You don't need to worry about that," he growls back at me and slams the door closed, the magick bouncing back into place.

I close my eyes and take a deep breath. "How did my life suddenly get so full of drama?" I ask, not expecting an answer.

"You married Aefre's daughter," To'Kah drawls, coming up behind me. He surprises me by dropping a light kiss on my lips. "That woman's life is one long soap opera."

I snort with amusement.

"What is a soap opera?" Pres asks.

I shake my head at him. "Never mind. Are we worried about this or not?" I point to the door.

"Not," To'Kah says. "Dracul won't do anything to harm her."

I fail to say, *except throw you in a pit of Dragon fire.*

"If you're sure?" Pres asks. "Because I have somewhere I need to be, and I need you both to come with me."

"Where to?" To'Kah asks.

"Where did you go earlier?" I ask him, ignoring Pres for a minute.

"To see Remiel, but he was with Dracul, so I didn't speak to him," he replies.

"What for?" I ask.

"We need to go. Now," Pres interrupts me.

"I'm glad you're okay," To'Kah whispers to me. "I knew it

was Trey the second I saw him with Delinda. I was worried about you."

"I'm okay," I say, feeling a rush of love for him. "He is messing with some serious evil. He got the jump on me."

Pres huffs and grabs me and To'Kah by the wrists and Astrals off to some kind of work room.

Aefre and Remiel are waiting for us, giving us looks of annoyance that we kept them waiting.

"Sorry," Pres says. "We were worried about Delinda."

"She's with Dracul," Remiel answers shortly.

"We know that now," Pres says.

"Why did you bring these two?" Aefre asks, gesturing at me and To'Kah.

"They need to know what's going on," Pres says.

"What *is* going on?" To'Kah asks.

"We are going to sever the Chosen bond and create a new connection between the four of us," Pres says. "Aefre said she can help."

"Hmm, what?" he says.

"Fill him in, would you?" Pres orders me and turns back to Aefre.

"Yes, sir," I drawl at him, but do as he says, anyway.

"How can you help?" Pres asks Aefre and Remiel, as I fill To'Kah in on our plan.

"You're going to sever the Chosen bond?" he whispers to me in shock, but I can see the shine of triumph in his eyes. He knows now he will have an equal footing with Delinda. If not a better one, because he's known her longer.

"What?" Pres exclaims.

I missed what they were saying as I filled To'Kah in.

"You can't do that!"

"Yes, we can. It's the quickest way to get the information we need," Aefre says. "Remiel can go to the Spirit Realm and bring her back."

"As a ghost?" Pres asks, looking as white as one.

I splutter and look between the two of them, standing

there so confident that this will work. "And who exactly are we bringing back from the dead?" I ask.

"My mother," Pres stutters.

"Oh?" To'Kah asks, coming forward his eyes boring into Aefre. "You know?"

"*You* know?" she spits at him.

"Know what?" I ask exasperated.

"His mother created the Chosen link between him and Delinda," Aefre says, shocking me to my core.

"EXCUSE ME?" I thunder at Pres, going for him, ready to pummel him into the ground. "You fabricated your bond to her? She was mine, all mine, all along, you fucker!"

Remiel slaps his hand to my chest to stop me from advancing further and it's like being hit by a ten-ton boulder. I struggle to take my next breath. "He did nothing of the sort. It was his mother. She died for her efforts."

"By you!" To'Kah points out viciously.

"Yes, I was the one that executed Shanti. She put my daughter in harm's way. That blood could have been used in a hundred different spells to hurt Delinda. It was treason."

I cast a glance at Pres. He is looking like he is going to puke.

"Besides, we are all here because she *isn't* just all yours, now, aren't we?" he continues with an icy blue glare at me.

I gulp. Well, he has me there. "Sorry," I mutter to Pres, who just nods dumbly at me.

"I knew something was up," To'Kah says to Remiel. "I was coming to find you to speak to you about it earlier."

"Oh?" Delinda's father snarls at him. "And what makes you think I would have seen you?"

"I also came to say thank you," he says softly.

"Humph," Remiel says rudely. "You live because of the child. Nothing more. You took advantage of my daughter and, for that, I will never accept you in her life."

I see Aefre put her hand on his arm to quiet him and it intrigues me. Usually she is the first to dive in with the hatred, but not now. "Go now and get Shanti. We need to get this done," she says to him quietly.

He nods once, grimly, and then disappears.

"How can he do that?" Pres asks.

"How can he do anything," Aefre replies with a shrug.

"What is Delinda talking to Dracul about?" I ask her.

"You will have to ask her that."

"That's nice and evasive," I mutter. To'Kah takes my hand and gives it a squeeze with a reassuring smile. I feel Aefre's eyes on us, but I don't dare to look at her.

I tear my eyes away from To'Kah to focus on Pres and I am surprised to see him going a bit doe eyed over Aefre.

I kick him in his shins. Hard. "What the fuck do you think you're doing?" I bark at him.

"It's not his fault," Aefre sighs. "The bond his mother made inadvertently included me as Delinda is of my blood."

"Oh, for fuck's sake. The longer you are in his presence, the stronger the bond gets," I spit out.

"Yep," she says, but seems completely unconcerned by it.

"If Delinda finds out about this…"

"She won't," Aefre says shortly. "She doesn't need to know about *any* of this. She will be heartbroken. We leave it that we severed the Chosen bond and created the Blood magick bond between you. She is already aware of the spell, so this won't come as a shock to her."

I nod, but I can't help feeling resentful. Pres was never meant to be a part of this. I must find it in me to get over it because it will do none of us any good to harbor these feelings. Remiel is right. We are here because it *still* went awry. There is still more than one Chosen One for her, it just happens to be every man in my family.

All I can think about now, is how I was supposed to be a triplet, but our other brother died before he hatched. Or at least, that is what we were told…there are so many secrets coming out now, who the fucks knows. Maybe he is still alive, and on his way here, to claim Delinda as well. I groan out loud as I think about that.

To'Kah and Pres give me a weird look, but I keep quiet. No one needs to know about this.

I am just about to ask where the Hell Remiel is, when he arrives back with a ghost which we all assume is Pres's mother.

22

~DELINDA~

I slump further into the sofa in my bedroom. I am crying so hard; I am glad my men aren't here to see it. I think this is what they call 'ugly crying'. Snot, tears and a scrunched-up face because I can't help it. I have never been a crier, up until my parents told me about my birth father. Then the floodgates opened. I am a sniveling mess, but Uncle D just leaves me to it.

"Delinda," he says kindly after what seems like forever of non-stop tears. "This is the way that it is."

"No!" I bawl at him. "I refuse to accept that. If that is what it takes, then I don't want it."

"You can't say that," he says.

I look up at him through my blurry eyes. He is sitting on the bed, directly opposite me, his elbows on his knees as he leans forward.

"This is *your* Power; you have to take it."

"Why did you lie to me before?" I shriek at him.

"I had to. I knew you would take it badly. I was waiting for the last moment to tell you."

"So basically, I was going to turn up at the ceremony and what? You were going to hand me the Dragon Slayers sword and say, 'do it'?" I scoff at him.

A small smile plays at his lips. "Something like that," he replies.

"Fantastic, thank you," I say stiffly, sniffing deeply and very grossly.

"Delinda, I am ready for this. I knew it when I made the decision to end my mother's reign of tyranny, that my days were numbered. This Power isn't mine. It was never meant to be mine. It is yours and you need to take it from me. You know that I would give it to you if I could, but that isn't how this works."

"You are my family!" I scream, rudely interrupting him. "You are as close to me as my parents. I can't do this. I can't kill you."

"I'm ready for this to end, Delinda," he says with a sigh. "I have lived for so long; I am ready to rest. You won't be doing anything I don't want you to do."

His words shock me to my core. "You *want* to die?"

"I want to rest," he says again. "I can't do that here. My life has been one long Power play, set up by my mother. Even with Her death. I am tired, girl. It is time for you to take what is yours and own it."

"I c-can't," I stammer at him. "I don't want to. I love you."

"I love you too, my precious child. But this is what it is. If you have any chance of rejecting the Chosen bond with Septimus, you need your full power."

"That's not fair! You can't throw that in my face to make me do this."

"I can, because it is true. He will not stop until he has you and control of these Realms. I can't allow either of those things to happen. I took the Power to keep it safe for you and to stop anyone else being able to take it from Her, and thus, you. This has all been about you, Delinda and the time has come. It is *past* time. I know this is difficult for you. You don't have it in you, but you have to dig deep, girl."

"I can't. I don't want to."

He sighs again. "I know it. You didn't even come at me when I threw your lover into the fire pit."

My eyes shoot up to his in an instant. "What?" I bark at him, the tears completely gone now. "You did that to get me to kill you?"

He gives me a lopsided half-smile, half-grimace. "I wasn't counting on Remiel saving him."

"How dare you!" I snarl at him. "You used him to get to me! That is completely unacceptable."

"He agreed to it," he states, which floors me in such a way, I hit the bottom of the ravine and keep on going.

"Excuse me?" I ask coldly, standing up, ignoring my spinning head.

"While you were grappling with your parents, I asked him what he wanted for you. If he knew what was required of you to take this Power. He knew. He also knew you wouldn't, couldn't, do it without provocation. So, we provoked you. Just not enough, apparently."

"Fuck you!" I hiss at him. "How dare you use him that way!" I am so angry; I could kill him.

Oh, wait. That's what he wants.

Oh, Jesus. I am so confused.

"You had no right, and neither did he, to make that decision for me. It is unforgivable."

"I did what I had to, and so did he. He was prepared to die for you to take your rightful place, Delinda. Don't you see how honorable that is?"

"*Honorable?*" I spit out. "It is selfish and stupid and dumb, and I am going to kick his ass so badly next time I see him!" I am shaking with rage, but also utter heartbreak. He was willing to sacrifice himself for me. How could he do that? How could he make that decision when we were happy and finally starting our life together?

The tears return and I sit back down.

"What will it take?" he asks me, just this side of nasty. "Do I need to go after your husbands? Is that the key here?"

"Don't even…" I growl at him, leaving that threat open-ended because he is doing this on purpose. "Don't think you can get away with this."

"I don't expect to, that's the whole point, Delinda," he says exasperated.

"You are infuriating!" I hiss at him.

"So are you, child. Just do it and be done with it!" He stands up now, towering over me as he glares down at me.

"I will find another way. There has to be a Power transfer spell."

"Not for *this* Power," he says, shaking his head. "How easy would that be for anyone to take it?"

Okay, he has a point.

"I'm not killing you," I state with finality.

"Then you won't be Empress! You won't take your rightful place, you will end up married to Septimus, and believe me when I say, you will suffer a fate worse than death as his wife. You will lose your husbands and your lover; he will kill them, even his own son. The child you are growing inside you will be executed as soon as it is born. He will control every aspect of your life; you will be a prisoner to his whims. He will try to kill me, repeatedly, and take this Power for himself. Is this what you really want, Delinda? A living Hell for us all?" He has completely lost his cool and is shouting at me. Telling me all of this horror that will befall me if I don't take what's mine.

"I will find another way," I say quietly and with a roar of frustration, he breaks the barrier and Astrals out, angrier than I have ever seen him.

I take a deep breath and close my eyes as I exhale. This has been a few days from Hell. How could two of the men I love most, conspire to get me to kill for this Power? It is…it is despicable. I am not sure I can forgive either one of them for this anytime soon.

I look up when I realize that I am not alone. But it isn't

anyone that I want to see in my doorway, and I gulp. I wish Uncle D had left the barrier up.

"What do you want?" I ask Septimus, standing up slowly to show him I'm not afraid of him.

"Isn't that obvious?" he asks me, his green eyes roving over me, making my skin crawl. "You are mine. I want you." He approaches me, striding forward and into my personal space with only a couple of steps.

"I belong to your son," I spit out, standing my ground, but pissed off that I have to tilt my head right back to look up at him. "There isn't a single part of my body, or heart, that he hasn't claimed."

Well, if I thought that would put him off—and I did—I am a bigger fool than Dracul thinks I am.

He laughs at me in delight. Ugh. "Now you are just turning me on," he says. "I don't have to think too hard about which parts of your body he has claimed." His eyes pin mine and I gulp. Uncle D was right about him. He is a complete sadist. I can see it in his eyes. He is looking forward to taking what belongs to his son and making it his. Probably in ways that even my wicked little imagination hasn't thought of. I take the coward's way out and attempt to Astral my ass out of there, but I don't go anywhere. Dammit, that is so fucking annoying. How does this dick have more power than me?

Err, the answer to that is obvious, of course. I know that, but it doesn't change anything. I am not killing my beloved uncle just to be stronger than this asshole.

"I am going to enjoy this," he murmurs, his eyes going back to taking in every inch of me.

I cross my arms over my chest, covering up my ample breasts as much as I can. This dress is stretchy and tight across my tits, just accentuating them even more. Which is normally something I favor, but not right now. I want to hide under a frumpy smock like the servant's wear.

He reaches out and grabs my arm, pulling it away from my chest, as well as dragging me closer to him. He tilts my chin up with his other hand, tightening his grip on me as I start to struggle. I bring my free hand up, complete with a hovering Dragon Orb on my palm, but he knocks my hand away, sending the Orb flying over to the bed to light it up in a small inferno.

He glances at it briefly, dousing it with just one thought, before he brings his gaze back to mine. "Is that any way to treat your Chosen One?"

"You aren't my Chosen One," I spit out. "Rex is. You will never have me." I am bold with my words, but he doesn't believe me.

"This bond is mine, Princess," he says, in a tone that suggests he is baffled that I could think otherwise. "What you feel with him is nothing compared to how I can make you feel."

"Ugh!" I cry out as he ducks his head to kiss me.

I shove him back, using every ounce of my Dragon-given strength and he stumbles, but only slightly. Shit, he is really strong. I have nothing left to use on him; it just won't work. The fear that I had of him, now turns into sheer panic. He can sense it and it makes him smile.

"That's intoxicating, Princess. I'd rather you accepted this, it would be so much more enjoyable for both of us, but if you are going to play it this way, I am fine with that."

His last five words are said in such a dark tone, I shudder.

I am about to forego all of my pride and scream my head off, when Dracul comes storming back into the room, full of rage and dragging Septimus away from me, with such force, I am surprised he didn't sever his arm.

"Touch her again, and you will wish for death," Uncle D snarls at him.

"You can't deny what we all know," Septimus replies. "She is mine and I will have her."

"If you even think about it, I will rip you to shreds and enjoy it," Papa growls at him from the doorway. His power has fired up and is a shimmering force around him.

Even Septimus, in his absolute arrogance, pauses to consider the threat from him.

I, on the other hand—and don't get me wrong, I am grateful to see my uncle and father stick up for me—am getting pissed the Hell off. I am supposed to be able to stick up for myself. No matter who it is against, I am supposed to be more powerful. More *Powerful*. With a capital P.

I see my father's eyes flick to mine, a fear growing as he shakes his head at me. I know the cause of his concern. My Light Fae powers are manifesting in my stress and anger, just like Mother said. I can see it myself, the white and gold dancing around my body, casting a glow in the darkening room as Papa's powers go into overdrive. I hope Mother doesn't turn up as well and start forming icicles on the ceiling. Things are tense enough as it is.

"I'd like to see you try, *nephew*," Septimus drawls, shaking himself from Dracul's grip.

I see Dracul's hand tighten again around Septimus, his eyes on me and my Fae powers. He is beyond pissed. Shit.

But then a feeling of sheer invincibility washes over me. As Powerful as I am with my Dragon at my back, this is something else. It's like I can get anyone to bend to my will. I suddenly remember this from mother's journals. The Light Fae royals have the power to coerce. Sebastian even used it on her to get her to stay with him. If I am his sister, then that makes me as powerful as he was.

Even though I haven't got a clue what I am doing, I reach out and grab Septimus's arm. He turns to me with a smug smile, thinking I am coming around to his way of thinking.

So do the other two men as they start to yell at me, but I ignore them and focus on the green eyes of the Dragon in front of me. "Leave," I state clearly. "Forget about the Chosen bond and go home."

He smirks at me and for a few seconds I think it didn't work. Shit. Now I have not only made a fool of myself, I have given away a set of powers that probably should have remained under wraps.

But then, he shakes his other arm out of Dracul's grip and nods, Astralling off without another word.

Err.

Am I the only one who thought that was too easy?

"What did you do?" Uncle D roars at me. "Did you just use your…" he looks around and lowers his roar to a whisper, "…Fae power on him."

"Yes," I state, sticking my chin in the air.

"Delinda! That kind of behavior is unacceptable under my roof!" He goes back to roaring.

"It worked, didn't it?" I ask him archly. Well, I *hope* it worked. "And this is *my* roof," I inform him, my father, my mother and everyone else that has come running to see what all the fuss is about. Including a ghostly looking woman that looks just like Pres.

"Delly," Mother says desperately. She can see that the Fae has taken over. "Be very careful what you do next," she warns me.

But I pay her no heed. I want the Power that is rightly mine. I don't want to rely on the power that my rapist birth father gave me to get what I want. If I can't even protect myself in the most basic way, what good am I to my family, to my unborn child?

I feel a breeze blowing my hair around my face. I brush the wisps aside and focus solely on Uncle D. He is glaring at me, but I think he gets what I am going to try to do. I am going to try to use these powers to rip my Power out of him and hope to fuck he doesn't die in the process.

"You can't do this," Mother whispers from right next to me. "You know nothing about these powers."

"Neither do you," I say to her, brushing her hand off my arm. "You don't have them."

"Delly, don't use them; this is a rabbit hole you don't want to go down."

Actually, it is. This power, having been bound and dormant for so long, is awake, and it wants me to lose myself in it.

"On your knees," I say to Uncle D, holding my hand out.

He shakes his head at me. "This isn't going to work."

"Do it!" I snap at him in a tone that won't be denied.

He sighs and shrugs and does as I ask, to mine, and everyone's disbelief.

If this doesn't work now, he is going to be so pissed at me that *I'll* probably end up in the fire pit.

"Delinda!" Mother whisper-snaps at me. "You cannot use your Fae power to take control of the Dragon Empire. You just can't!"

I ignore her.

"Let her try," Uncle D says, resigned.

That stops her, and me, in our tracks.

She brushes it off quickly. "You cannot bend the Power to your will," she whispers urgently.

"I am trying and that's final," I state and place my hand on Uncle D's head, closing my eyes and gathering the strength that I need.

"If this doesn't work, then you do this *my* way. Tomorrow," Uncle D growls at me.

Well, if it wasn't enough of an incentive to get rid of Rex's dad, then that threat certainly was.

I dig deep.

Really deep.

Do it.

I scrunch my eyes up tighter.

Do it.

Who is that? It's coming from inside my head. Is the power talking to me? Or have I completely lost my mind.

Use me to get what you want.

Okay, now it's freaking me out. Do Mother's powers talk to her? Or is this a Light Fae thing?

I channel the power. I can feel it coursing through my veins at a rapid rate.

I know everyone is staring at me, but I try not to let that put me off.

Use me and I can give you everything you desire.

"Stop it," I mumble out loud.

"Who is she talking to?" I hear Rex ask. "And what the Hell is that glow coming from her?"

I hear Mother gasp next to me and then tell them to get out. She knows it's too late. I am going to have to come clean about the Fae Powers now.

I want to be used, Delinda. I need it. Use me and you will never be vulnerable again.

I pay heed this time and talk back to it in my head.

Give me this and I will use you every day, I swear. I will not let you go dormant or be squashed down ever again. Just give me this and I swear I will give you what you want.

I know this is what it wants to hear.

I hear a low buzzing noise and the wind amps up, swirling around us now as Mother tries to stop me once again. But I won't be denied now. This power *will not* be denied. It is out in full force, a blinding gold and white light that I can see, even though my eyes are shut.

Everyone in the room is crying out from the sheer force and light coming out of my hand as I pull the Power out of Uncle D.

My hand is aching. It is outstretched, my fingers hooked into claws as I pull and pull at the Power. I am absorbing it as quickly as it is coming out. It is like ice in my veins in contrast to the white-hot heat from the Fae magick.

"Shit," Mother cries. "Remiel! Do something!"

"Leave her," he says to her. "We can't stop her now."

"What the fucking Hell is she doing?" Rex thunders, but it all just sound like background noise to me.

The only thing that matters is finishing what I started.

What we *started, Princess.*

I flinch, but carry on, pulling and pulling. I am pushing down so hard, Uncle D grunts in pain, but I still haven't finished. The Power is coming to me. It wants to be here, but the internal struggle with the Fae magick is making it difficult to concentrate. Neither one of them wants the other there. It is a battle just to stay standing as the war rages inside me as more and more of the Power of the Dragon Empire goes into me.

Princess!

The voice sounds oddly human now, as opposed to the sickly-sweet melody that it was before.

Finish it and we can be as one.

"AAAAAHHHH!" I cry out as the force of the Dragon Power hits me so hard, I stumble, dropping to my knees exhausted, but I'm not finished yet.

Take me. Say I am yours.

"Mine!" I shout out. "You are fucking mine now finish this!"

I am slammed to my back on the cold stone floor, shuddering so violently as She claws at me again and again. I know She is trying to oust the Fae power, but it isn't going anywhere. I don't want it to. I want to keep it right where it is.

That's it, Princess. Let it take you over.

I stop shuddering and She stills just as suddenly as she started.

Come to me, Princess. Come and find me.

"I will," I mumble, my mouth as dry as the Sahara. "I will."

I sink into oblivion knowing that whoever it was that helped me, had access to my powers and gave it a kick up the ass like I have never borne witness to before. I know now that it was a sentient being talking to me, not the power. I know it was a 'he'. I *know* that I must find him.

23
~TO'KAH~

The room has fallen into complete silence. No one is even breathing. We are all shocked to our very cores about what we just saw here. I have no concept what that was, but Delinda somehow *pulled* the Power out of her uncle and absorbed it in a bright white and gold light. I have never seen Dragon magick that color before. It was beautiful, just like she is. I suppose it makes sense that her magick is different. She is a Gold Dragon. The only one of Her kind.

I look at Aefre and Remiel. They are gripping each other, their faces pale as they stare at their daughter, prone on the floor.

I'm the one that leaps into action.

Delinda is starting to shudder again, which signifies She is agitated. I lunge forward and scoop her up off the floor. Everyone else takes a breath and starts to move again.

I cast a glance at Dracul.

He looks dead.

If Delinda killed him, she will never get over it.

I look away and place her on the bed, turning her onto her side so that I have access to her back. Her dress has been clawed by the Dragon; it is in shreds. I tear the remains away from her nape to her waist and put my hand flat on her back.

The Dragon is swooping violently across her back, scraping her skin, but not slashing at her anymore.

"Is the Emperor alive?" I ask quietly, turning my hand over and then running the back of my hand gently over Her. She calms instantly, flying in a circle and then coming to rest in the middle of Delinda's back, with her eyes closed. I continue to stroke her as Remiel lets go of Aefre and crosses over to Dracul.

Aefre walks over to me, staring down at her daughter.

"He's alive," Remiel states. "Barely."

"He's not the Emperor anymore," Aefre whispers.

It stuns the room back into silence.

I mean, we all *knew* that was the Power that crossed over between uncle and niece, but it hadn't sunk in until now.

Delinda is the Empress.

She claimed the throne in a way that will leave no one in any doubt as to her strength and her Power, but also her mercifulness. She didn't kill to take the Power.

She found another way.

"I'll take Dracul to his room, make him more comfortable," Remiel says, scooping him up and Astralling away.

"Come here," I order Delinda's two husbands. "Take her hands."

Rex is there in a flash, gently picking her hand up and kissing it.

Pres is slower to approach. His mother has disappeared, probably not able to be here for very long, without Remiel's power to tie her to this Realm.

I make a 'hurry up' gesture to him and he hastens, picking her hand up and sinking to his knees on the floor next to Rex.

It suddenly strikes me why they can't soothe Her in the way that a Chosen One is supposed to. Rex's bond to her is inherited and, thus, weaker and Pres's was completely fabricated. It is enough to fool the Dragon when She is happy, but when She gets agitated, She is seeking something that just isn't there.

It never will be.

I will be in Her life for eternity now and that makes me smile to myself. She will always need *me*.

I continue to stroke Her, but She is at peace now, so I risk taking my hand off Her. I will need to balance that Power soon, but I will wait until Delinda wakes. She will want to experience it; I have no doubt.

"The-the baby?" Aefre croaks out.

"I don't know," I say quietly.

"Move," she orders the three of us and we go without question. This is far more important than Aefre's attitude.

She rolls Delinda onto her back and places her hand, low down on her stomach. She closes her eyes and we wait.

We wait so long, that Remiel returns and joins her, clasping her hand to give her a boost of his extra special mojo.

She hisses and pulls her hand back as she is burned by the visible sparks of electricity.

She gives me a relieved smile and my heart thumps.

"Baby is just fine," she says, placing her hand on my arm in a kind gesture that makes me stare at it, moved, before I am roughly shoved away by Remiel.

"Thank you," I say quietly and then dismiss her to go back to Delinda's side.

"We'll leave you for a bit," Aefre says. "Call us the second she wakes."

"We will," Rex says.

Remiel protests at volume. "I am not leaving her!"

"Yes, we are," Aefre says, taking his hand. "She is being taken care of."

He grimaces at her, but she ignores him and looks at me. "As. Soon. As. She. Wakes. Up." She jabs her finger at me with each word.

I nod and say, "Yes, of course."

Then they Astral off and leaves us alone.

"What the fuck was that?" Rex demands as soon as they have gone. "What was that power she used? I have never seen anything like that before and I have been around a fucking long time."

"F-Fae magick," Pres stammers, not looking up from his wife's face.

"Don't be absurd," Rex scoffs. "She has no Dark Fae in her whatsoever."

But the dubious look he gives her, doesn't back up his words.

"I would know if she did," I say confidently. "I have never seen her use any of the magick that Aefre uses."

"I'm telling you, it's Fae magick," Pres rounds on us, growling like a rabid dog.

"How would you even know?" Rex snaps back at him. "You have barely lived, never mind lived anywhere near the Fae."

"I know. My mother taught me everything about the different kinds of magick. White and gold. That's Fae. *Light* Fae," Pres says with such authority that Rex and I gulp and look at each other.

"Light Fae? No, that can't be right," I insist, brushing the doubt aside. "Aefre is half *Dark* Fae. She has no Light Fae in her lineage."

"How do you know so much about her?" Pres asks.

"Jealous?" Rex snaps at him and turns back to me. "Are you sure?"

"Absolutely," I grit out, giving Pres a hard look. That connection between him and Delinda, which includes Aefre, needs to be severed. Now. If Delinda finds out…

"So that means…what, exactly?" Rex asks. "Remiel isn't Fae at all."

"Maybe he is," Pres says. "What do we really know about him?"

I roll my eyes at him. His naivety is showing. "He is completely un-Fae. Trust me on that."

"So, what then?" Rex presses.

The three of us look at each other.

I can see the realization hit us.

We land on the only conclusion we can.

"Remiel isn't her real father," I state in a hushed tone.

"How can that be?" Pres asks.

I blink. Then I start to sweat. Aefre was involved with the Light Fae when she found out about her father. She suffered there, right before Tiamat gave her full Powers to her. I was there when that happened. I know, or at least, I overheard some things and put two and two together. "She was raped by the Light Fae King twenty-three years ago," I whisper, looking at Delinda. It all makes so much sense now, why she looks nothing like Remiel. She bares absolutely none of his features, none of his coloring. "She was already pregnant during her heat when Remiel was meant to breed with her."

"It bothers me that you know all of this," Rex spits out, arms folded across his chest tightly.

"I was her Guardian, for fuck's sake," I spit back. "I know a lot about her that I wish I didn't."

"And yet, it never occurred to you before now?"

"Obviously not. Remiel took her during her heat, she fell pregnant, gave birth to the child here and that was it. There was no reason to believe it happened any other way."

"Do you think they know?" Pres asks a really dumb question.

"Of course they do!" I exclaim. "They have been protecting her. Aefre must've bound her powers when she came to live here permanently. She knew it would affect Delinda's authority if she was half Fae, and not the daughter of The Queen and her Chosen One."

"Do you think Dracul knew?" he asks with a frown.

"*Knows*," I point out. "He isn't dead. Yet." I add, shaking my head. "Yes, he must've known."

"So why the sudden reappearance of her powers?" Rex asks, glaring down at his wife with immense anger on his face.

"Aefre unbound them for some reason. Who knows why, and why now?"

"Fuck!" Rex roars. "She is…I knew she wasn't a pureblood, but *this*…this is a disgrace."

"Calm down," I tell Rex as She is getting riled up by the tension in the air. Although, I have to agree. It is the worst thing that could possibly have happened. I don't even know what I am going to say to her when she wakes up, but right now, she needs us to keep our traps shut about what we saw until, *if*, she decides to tell everyone she is half Fae.

24

~PRES~

This is bad. Really bad. I don't know how I feel about my wife being half of the creature I was taught to loathe. In fact, *all* Dragons loathe the Fae. The history is long and messy and, all Tiamat's fault, but still...if our Empress said we hate them, then we hate them. Simple. I wonder if Delinda will want to make amends now that *she* is Empress.

"Pres?"

"Hmm, what?" I ask, still in a daze.

Rex glares at me. "I asked if you got what you needed from your mother before she disappeared?"

"Rex," To'Kah says gently. "Get how upsetting that must've been for him."

I throw him a grateful smile.

"Sorry," Rex mumbles. "But did you?"

He is pacing up and down, and now that I've noticed, it is irritating me. "Will you stop?" I ask him. "It's not helping the tension in here."

"He's right," To'Kah agrees with me.

Rex stops and gives him a vicious growl. "My wife has been lying to me about something pretty fucking huge, so you'll forgive me if I'm a bit stressed about it."

"She's lied to all of us," To'Kah points out. "You know that if she wakes up now and you go at her in the state you are currently in, it will end badly for you, and probably us too."

He is not wrong. Delly will kick his ass if he starts accusing her of lying on top of being a Fae.

"Look, if she knows who her father is, if Aefre told her how she was conceived, she will be very upset about that. The last thing she needs is us coming at her *at all*. We let her do this her way. If she wants to explain, then fine, if not, we leave it," To'Kah says, being the voice of reason.

"I agree," I state. "I am pissed that she has lied about this, but I can understand why. She has no reason at all why admitting to her heritage would be a good thing. In fact, it is the opposite. She has everything to lose. Rex?" I press when he doesn't say anything.

"Fine," he mutters. "I know the shame of being conceived in a less than romantic way."

I gape at him, as To'Kah gives him a sympathetic look and reaches out to grab his hand as Rex paces past him again.

"She is still the True Heir to this Empire, no matter what else she is now," To'Kah says. "Aefre is still her mother. She will just have a small struggle on her hands now to be fully accepted it she decides to tell everyone her secret. We are here to support her no matter what our own feelings are about this. We must give her a chance to explain before we accuse her. We let her know how we feel about it and then we drop it. Got it?"

I nod. I want to have my say on this, but I also don't want her hating me and telling me to get lost. Seeing what she did, the sheer power she has, regardless of it being backed up by the Fae in her, was spectacular. *She* is spectacular. I love her more than I ever thought possible, even though I'm not pleased about this development.

"We still need to do this severing thing," Rex blurts out into the silence that falls.

"We will. As soon as we have discussed it with her. She is

our Empress now. We will respect that," To'Kah says with a reverent look at her.

It makes me and Rex look at her with growing awe as well.

"Shit, we are married to the Empress," I whisper.

"Speak for yourself," To'Kah drawls.

"Sorry," I mumble at him, "but you know now she will make it official."

He remains silent so I don't think he heard me.

"Yeah, maybe," he says eventually.

"She will," Rex says, finally stopping his pacing and coming to crouch next to To'Kah. "She loves you."

"I love her," he states.

It sounds like he is trying to convince himself that he still does.

The mood goes even more somber after that comment.

Time ticks away and she doesn't awake. I am starting to get really worried.

To distract myself, I grab a pen and a piece of paper and start to work on the severing spell.

My mother did give me everything I needed to perform this spell, including a damn good reason why I *need* to. She whispered it to me when everyone else was watching Delinda extract the Power out of Dracul. My connection to her has a time limit. My mother never factored into the spell, or the decision behind it, that Delinda would end up with multiple partners. She expected for me to be Chosen and for me to impregnate Delinda shortly after our marriage. She was sure that would solidify the bond. But, of course, she isn't pregnant with my child. I am sure about that even if she has doubts as to who the child's father is. The false connection is going to wither away without something to tie us together. I need to cut that connection before Delinda feels what it's like to be without me.

These two spells must be done in rapid succession, so everything has to be perfect.

"You got this?" Rex mutters to me, peering over my shoulder.

"Yeah, I think so. It's the timing that's going to be the hardest part. I have to get this just right."

"What do you mean?"

I hesitate, but then I say, "I don't want Delinda to feel the loss of the Chosen bond with me, us, even for a second. I have to perform the spells quickly, or even better, simultaneously. It's going to be tricky."

Rex's eyes go wide and then narrow. "How can I help?" he asks, having come up with the exact same possibility that I did: that if she knows she doesn't have a bond to us, she will ditch us and run off with To'Kah. The man that she loved long before we came along.

"How are you with magick?" I ask.

He shrugs. "Adequate."

"Can you hold a Black magick spell for about a minute?" I wait for his reaction to that.

"If that is what it takes," he states with absolute conviction.

I nod, knowing that he will do whatever he can to ensure the Chosen connection is broken, *after* the tie-to-life spell starts.

"Now all we need is for her to wake up," I say, looking back at her while shoving my notes over to Rex.

He glances at it and then hunches his shoulders as he realizes it is the spell that he must start while I finish the severing spell.

"How safe is this?" he asks me.

"I dunno. We could ask Aefre. She performed this spell with her husbands."

Rex's eyes shoot to mine. "I don't fucking think so, kid. You stay the fuck away from her."

I grimace at him. "I'm not in love with her or anything."

"Whatever you are, is enough to piss the shit out of Delinda if she finds out about it. *That* is enough to know it's wrong if you can't see it otherwise."

My face nearly folds in on itself, I frown at him so hard. "I know it's wrong, you asshat. But not my fault," I grit out.

He smirks at me and my insult. "Oh, we'll make an Alpha out of you, yet."

"No, thanks," Delinda says, startling us both. "I've got enough of those in my life already."

25

~DELINDA~

I bat my lashes at my two husbands and then tilt my face towards To'Kah as he bends to kiss me. It's on my cheek, chaste and quick. I give him a puzzled look, but he is avoiding my eyes.

I gulp as the other two men are doing the same.

"I see," I say with as much dignity as I can, climbing off the bed and fixing my torn dress with magick. "I am no longer desirable to you now that you know my secret."

"It's not that," To'Kah starts, but he still isn't looking at me.

"It's that I didn't tell you?"

"Yeah," Rex says.

I can see him trying desperately to hold on to his temper. "We figured it all out, Delinda."

I gulp. *All* of it? That's not good.

"Nothing to say?" he barks at me.

"Rex," To'Kah warns him.

I see him button it and I sigh.

"I'm sorry. I know I should have said something, but I only just found out a few days ago. Well, about who my father really was and how I was conceived." I pin To'Kah's eyes. "You knew what happened to my mother?

"Yes," he says, coming to me slowly. "I was her Guardian at that time."

"Never thought to share?" I ask nastily, just to turn the tables on him.

His eyes go really dark as he finally looks at me. "That is not fair, Princess," he growls.

I give him a smug, arrogant look and he realizes his mistake.

"That's *Empress*, to you," I spit out.

He lowers his eyes again and does something that surprises me. I expected, needed him to come at me, guns blazing, to get this off his chest, but he does the opposite. He drops to his knees, his head bowed in supplication. I gape at them as the other two do the same.

"Yes, Your Highness," they murmur at me.

"Get up, you idiots," I huff at them. I don't like seeing them bow down to me. I am their woman. They don't owe me this. Especially now.

"Is Dracul okay?" I croak out in the silence that follows after they obey me.

"He's alive," To'Kah says briskly. "Your father took him back to his room to recuperate."

Time seems to stop as we all register what he said.

"Remiel," he chokes out. "Remiel took him back to his room."

It gets my back up in the worst way. I feel the fire in my eyes and the talons extend. The wings of my Dragon have sprouted and the look of sheer terror on the face of my lover only serves to ignite the sudden aggression that has risen up. "Remiel is my father!" I boom at him. "If I hear any one of you say otherwise, I will make you regret it in ways that will give you nightmares!"

"I'm sorry," To'Kah rushes to say. "I didn't..."

He stops talking as I screech at him. I have transformed into some hybrid, half-human, half-Dragon creature and it is scaring the shit out of me, never mind the three men cowering in front of me. Pres looks like he is about to pass out.

I take a deep breath and close my eyes. I focus on what To'Kah said. Uncle D is going to be okay. I took the Power, and I didn't have to kill him for it. The relief that floods me, transforms me back into my human form and I open my eyes.

I look at To'Kah. "I'm sorry that I didn't tell you. All of you." I include Rex and Pres in my apologetic look. "You have to understand that it had to be kept a secret. I have always known that Remiel wasn't my birth father, but my mother never told me who he was. She refused. I learned why only a few days ago. That night we met on the terrace," I add to Rex, so he knows just how recent. "I only found out I was half Light Fae a few months ago. My mother had bound my powers and took my memories away. She knew that living here, I needed it suppressed. I am still dealing with finding out who my birth father is. Please understand that I would have mentioned it, I just needed time to deal with it first." I say the lie easily because it is what they want to hear. What they *need* to hear.

"I can get past the not telling," Pres blurts out. "But *Fae*? Delinda, you are half of everything that we have been taught to despise."

"Only because Tiamat fucked up and alienated them. The Fae once lived in harmony with the Dragons until She tried to control them. I can change things; I can change the perspective."

"So they will accept you?" To'Kah spits out at me, the venom in his voice making my heart thump. "I understand everything you have told us, but it doesn't change the fact that you are half Fae. I am not sure how I will get past this. The thought of that magick touching Her disgusts me."

I gasp at his words. He might as well have struck me.

"That you just used that power to take control of the Dragon Empire, makes me sick to my stomach," he carries on, as if he hasn't done enough damage to my heart already. "I don't want Her anywhere near that reviled creature inside you. And don't even get me started on my child!"

He stops talking as Rex hisses at him to shut it. But it's too late. It's been said, and he can't take it back even if he backtracks.

Which he doesn't.

"I see," I say coldly. "You hold it against me that I was conceived during a rape."

His face softens a fraction. "That's not fair, Delly."

"Neither is what you are saying. I didn't have a choice in this. It is what it is."

"Ask your mother to bind the powers again," he says to me, approaching me cautiously. "You can get rid of them and you can rule as a Dragon. The Dragon doesn't have to share you."

"No," I state. "I will not bind these powers. You can either accept me as I am now, or the door is behind you and don't let it hit you on the way out."

I turn from them, devastated that he finds me so repulsive. Not to mention, the other two haven't had their say yet. "Decide now."

I hear the door thump and my broken heart smashes into a million more pieces.

"I am not leaving you, you silly girl," Rex snaps at me. "But you do have some making up to do."

I turn to him quickly, to see that Pres is also still in the room.

I give them a watery smile. "You don't find me repulsive?" I sob.

Rex smiles gently. "No. I'm not happy about this development, or the fact that you kept it to yourself. I *do* understand why you kept it a secret at large. But from *us*?"

"I'm sorry," I bleat.

He sighs and comes to me, scooping me up in a big hug. "I forgive you, on one condition. You will not keep anything to yourself ever again. We are a team now, Princess, uhm,

Empress." He shakes his head. "That sounds too weird. We are here to help you deal with your shit, no matter what it is."

"Done," I weep into his shirt and then pull myself together. I push him away and look at Pres, still looking at me like he lost his best friend.

"Have your say," I say stiffly, straightening my back and ready to take it on the chin now that I have Rex's support.

His eyes search mine. "I have only ever known one way. We hate the Fae. But I love you, Delinda. It is confusing."

"I know," I say quietly.

"My mother taught me a lot about the Fae. There is still something you aren't telling us. You get one chance to come completely clean."

I stare at him in shock. Where did those balls come from?

"One chance, or I leave."

Well, Jesus. It's not like I have a choice now is it. When I told them if they couldn't accept me, then they should go, it was a bluff. Only To'Kah took me at my word and fucked off, taking my heart with him. I can't lose another of my men over this. I'm going to have to tell them.

"Delinda?" Rex asks me with a frown. "What is he talking about?"

"My mother is the Dark Fae Princess," I croak out. "The only one. I was born to her by the Light Fae King. The only child to be born from the two races. I am the True Heir here, but I am also the Blessed child, or whatever they call me, over there."

"What?" Rex asks, shaking his head in confusion. "You are meant to rule there as well?"

"Err, not sure as to my role. Mother hasn't told me much." I look down, embarrassed.

"And?" Pres barks at me.

I look up at him, puzzled. "That's it. That's all I know. I swear."

"We heard you talking to him," Pres states icily.

"What?" I ask, squinting at him.

"You are fucking mine, now finish this," he says.

I blink at him as it hits me. "Uhm," I say, my cheeks now flaming.

"What is he talking about?" Rex snaps at me.

"I may have made the connection with my Fae mate," I say and brace myself for the backlash of anger that, indeed, comes my way.

26

~REX~

"Are you fucking serious?" I snarl at her.

"Yes," she squeaks. "It was inadvertent. I can only imagine he felt me use the power to that degree and latched onto it."

"Oh, did he now," I drawl, the sarcasm so thick you could hack away at it with a sword.

"Who is he?" Pres croaks out.

"I have no idea!" she exclaims. "Mother mentioned something about a Fae mate, but I didn't take her seriously, nor did I have any hope of pursuing it to see if she meant it!"

Her exacerbation is genuine. She truly didn't know about this Fae fucker until the Power transfer.

"And will you now?" Pres asks.

He is cold and hard. It is the first time I have ever seen him this way. It's kinda turning me on. If this weren't such a fucking travesty, I would suggest we postpone this godawful chat and head to bed.

"No!" she states firmly. "My place is *here*. I am Empress now. I will not abandon that post for a man I know nothing about. I am a Dragon first and foremost. I always have been, and this changes nothing." She lifts her chin up defiantly, which makes me think she isn't being entirely honest about that.

...nor did I have any intention of pursuing it.

Did I.

Does that mean she does now?

"It does though," Pres insists. "It changes everything."

"No, it doesn't," she argues. "He can't get here, and I am not leaving. I want nothing to do with my rapist father's people!"

Oh, nice. She knows how to hit it where it hurts. Pres's face has crumpled like a piece of tissue paper at that reminder.

"You have to trust me, or this isn't going to work," she says, her bottom lip quivering slightly. "Do you trust me, husband?"

That is his complete undoing. I roll my eyes as he goes to her, swooping down on her to kiss her soundly.

"Of course, I do," he says firmly. "I just needed to hear you say these things."

She gives him a loving smile that has him practically coming in his pants.

I sigh. So much for him becoming an Alpha. She has him right where she wants him. She has played him like a fiddle.

"Do you trust me?" she asks me, her eyes shrewd.

"Are you telling us the truth?" I challenge her, giving her a shrewd look back that she can't get away from.

She squirms slightly but masks it as her trying to get away from Pres to come to me.

"Of course I am. I love you. I would never do anything to hurt either one of you."

It's what I want to hear, but I am not as easy to manipulate as her Beta husband. She knows that and runs her hands up my chest. She fists her hands in my shirt and drags me to her for a kiss that is made for distracting.

It does what it's meant to.

I go hard and grab her ass, squeezing tightly. I want to say that I trust her—I love her—but I don't trust her. At least not about this Fae mate. She had no intention of telling us. It was only when Pres pushed it, that she caved.

She unbuttons my shirt and pushes it off my shoulders. It slides to the floor and just as I think I have gotten away with it, she asks me again, "Do you trust me?"

If I say no now, she will stop what she is doing, and I really don't want that. This day has been fraught with Trey, my father, nearly being burned alive, the Power transfer and now this Fae thing. I need this. I need her.

"Yes," I say, just to keep her doing what she is doing.

She smiles that glorious smile at me and drops to her knees to undo my pants. They drop around my ankles and she says, "Will you speak to To'Kah? Make him see reason?"

"Yes," I say, because now she has my dick in her mouth. I will say yes to absolutely anything as she sucks me hard, grazing me with her teeth in that way that makes me explode in her mouth before I know what's hit me.

"Fuck," I grunt, shooting my load down her throat, my hand fisting in her hair.

The only thing I can do now, is keep a watchful eye on her, and make her know that I'm watching her every move. She has one thing going for her. The Fae can't get here. But she can come and go as she pleases. We just have to make sure that she doesn't feel the need to go off and pursue this asshole that has slid into her life in such an insidious way, it makes me sick.

27
~TO'KAH~

My heart is broken. I thought she would fight harder than that to keep me. I pushed her too hard. I know that, but I was, I *am* upset, disgusted and angry. How can I just overlook this? It isn't what is best for Her and She is *my* concern.

I hoped the other men would follow me, to show her we are united in this, but I shouldn't be surprised that they stayed. They have the Chosen bond to her, no matter how they got it, it's there. I don't have that with her. She isn't able to sway me as she can the others. They are probably banging away inside her even now, while I sit here wallowing in my self-pity. I should be more reasonable about this, but after what the Fae did to Aefre, I just can't. I saw her right after it happened. She had her Powers bound, and she was helpless. She looked so vulnerable and sad; it broke my heart. I can't help that, even after everything, it still affects me. The fact that Delinda is the product of that rape makes me want to vomit and never stop.

It is only now that I stop thinking about myself and start thinking about her.

"Jesus," I mutter. I have been a complete dick. How could

I abandon her? How could I abandon *Her*? I'm going to have to dig deep and push the disgust that I feel for her Fae half aside. I want to be with her. I can't leave her. There is just no way, now that we are officially together, that I can *not* be with her. I love her. I adore her and my destiny is intertwined with Hers. Somehow, I have to convince her that I can accept this, and maybe, over time, I will.

I turn around and head back to the bedroom on foot. One thing is very clear, Delinda needs our support now more than ever. She has taken on the Empire with absolutely no idea what that entails. It is going to take all of us to help her figure it out without anyone else finding out that she isn't ready for this responsibility. I need to put my own feelings aside and focus solely on Delinda and her other two men. We will need to be there for each other, so that we can stay strong in front of Delinda. Pres especially is going to need me and Rex to take some of the burden of being the Empress's husband off him.

I push open the bedroom door, and, as expected, find the three of them in a tangle on the bed. I tilt my head to the side, to try to figure out who is where. All I can see are limbs and asses.

"You're back?" Rex asks, daring me to say anything except 'yes'.

"Yes."

Turning over, he pounds into Delinda so hard she screams.

"Is there something you want to say to our Empress?" he asks.

The room goes quiet and Delinda sits up, giving me a really hurt look.

"I was an asshole, and I apologize. I spoke in anger and hurt, but it was wrong of me. I love you and support you, Delly. You know that."

Her face softens, and she smiles at me, holding her hand out for me to join them.

I hesitate for only a second. I can do this. I can love her like she deserves to be loved. The Fae in her can be squashed again. I will talk to Aefre and Remiel; make them see that this isn't what is best for their daughter. With that decided, I climb onto the bed.

28

~DELINDA~

*O*nce again, the three men have crashed after a fuck session that has left me reassured and feeling the love. I was really worried that they wouldn't accept me. When To'Kah left, I was sure he wouldn't come back, and then Pres pushed me into saying the very thing I was going to keep quiet. I sigh and climb off the bed.

I head to the bathroom and duck quickly into the shower. I clean up, then Astral myself dry and dressed, and then send myself straight to my parents. We need to talk in a big way.

I find them in Uncle D's room, which is weird. I have never been in here. I suppose it was incredibly rude of me. They could have been doing anything, and I just thought about me and Astralled in.

"Delly!" Mother cries and crushes me in a fierce hug.

Papa is more restrained in his greeting but no less happy to see me.

"You are in so much trouble!" Mother scolds me, after a minute of hugging.

"Don't I know it," I whine and look at Uncle D, still lying unconscious on the bed. "It just flared up and then I knew I could get the Power this way."

"Your husbands…" She bites her lip, worried.

"They know," I sigh and fix her with a vicious glare. "And To'Kah filled in the blanks. You were a lot closer than he let on." This hurts me but I know I must push it away. He loves *me*. I have to keep remembering that.

She looks away. "He was my Guardian," she says quietly. "I can't help that. What did they say?"

"They all had a go, but we're okay now," I state.

"Are you?" she asks carefully.

I give her a curious look. "Yes. They were angry, but we made up."

Her face goes slightly green. "Hmm," she murmurs. Then, "How long have you been awake?"

"A couple of hours," I get out before she starts yelling at me.

"I told them to get us as soon as you woke up!"

"We had shit to sort out. They were seriously pissed about the Fae thing, but even more so that I lied to them."

"Do they know about your Fae mate?" Mother asks me, pinning my eyes with her laser-like ones.

"Rex and Pres do. To'Kah doesn't know yet," I admit. I must rectify that immediately. If he hears about it from my husbands first, he will probably leave for good. Hopefully they know that and will leave me to mention it. "How do *you* know about my Fae mate?"

"Oh, please," she scoffs. "It was kind of obvious that you had help. Big, bad help."

I take offense at that. "You don't think I could do this on my own?" I ask haughtily.

"No," she states being brutally honest, with her arms folded. "You are still young and not trained enough in your Dragon Powers, never mind your Fae ones, to accomplish this on your own." She indicates Uncle D's prone form.

I silently fume at her, looking at Papa for the support I need.

I don't get it.

135

He is being silent for a damn good reason. He is so pissed off; he looks like he is about to explode.

"I'm sorry," I whisper to him. "I know how this affects you too."

Mother looks between us and goes to him to grab his hand.

"They won't tell. I swear it," I say to him, also going to him and giving him an awkward hug because Mother doesn't let him go.

"This isn't about me," he says. "This has always been about protecting you, Delinda. I think we need to re-bind your Fae powers."

"What?" I rear back from him, incredulous. "You can't do that! You can't deny half of who I am!"

His pained look, and Mother's gasp, make me realize what I said, and it was horrid and hurtful. I have accepted what my birth father has given to me.

"I think it's for the best," Mother says, quietly. "You can't rule here with the Fae rearing its head. You will be shunned."

"I am Empress!" I state with dignity. "They cannot shun me."

"Oh, they can," Uncle D croaks behind me.

The three of us spin around and go to him. I take his hand, but he drags it out of my reach. I pull back like I have been burned and fold my hands behind me. He can't bear to even look at me after what I did to him.

I gulp.

What have I done?

What you had to. You couldn't kill him outright.

My inner voice has a point, but it doesn't make me feel any better.

"They will turn from you; you will face contempt and a coup for your Power. And you are aware exactly how that will happen."

Mother hisses at him, but he stands up, shakily, and

pushes past her to cross to the other side of the room. Only then he turns to face me.

"I don't know how long that mind-trick you pulled on Septimus will last, but once it wears off, he will be back, and he will take what he thinks is his. You aren't strong enough in your current state to beat him if he comes at you with his full power, Delinda. I won't be able to protect you as I should with the way that I am now. He is ancient and a Dragon Prince. Yes, you are Empress, but you aren't ready for a coup, trust me on that."

Papa growls at him but gets ignored.

I stand there, chastised and humiliated. They all think I am too weak to hold this title, this Power. It is humbling and I wonder if I have made a huge mistake.

"I can do this with the Fae power," I say. "It makes me stronger."

"It will be your end," Uncle D says and Astrals out leaving the three of us to stare at each other, in a growing atmosphere, that leaves me with no doubt that my parents are already plotting to squash my Fae side again.

Over my dead body.

And mine, Princess.

29

~REX~

I awake to find Delinda gone. I sit upright and scan the room. She is standing at the window, looking out over the cliff tops. If she hears me stir, she doesn't look around. Her tight stance and grim face give a big, glaring warning to approach with caution.

"Hey." A nice simple, inoffensive greeting.

"Hey," she says back, but nothing else.

"Want to talk about it?" I ask carefully.

"My parents and uncle want to bind my Fae powers. They think the Dragons will shun me and start planning a coup."

I want to tell her that they aren't wrong, but that will get me a kick in the ass out of the door, I am sure.

"You agree with them, don't you?" She turns to look at me earnestly. "Speak freely," she clips out.

"Yes," I say, hoping she meant it. "If you want to keep the powers, then you need to hide them. You cannot let any other Dragon see you use them."

She sighs and her shoulders slump. "I want to explore them," she says mutinously.

She just isn't getting it. It's time for tough love and damn the consequences. "Why would you want anything to do with the powers that your rapist father gave you? Not only is that a punch in the face to your mother, especially, but your father as well. It is giving *him* power over you."

"He's dead."

"So what?" I ask incredulously. "He will live on forever if you continue to not only keep the powers but use them. That is not what your parents want for you. It isn't what we want for you."

"You are just worried about the Fae mate," she snaps at me dismissively.

"While it is a concern, you said that you wouldn't pursue it," I point out, wishing that I didn't have to.

She glares at me, those green eyes filled with anger and pain.

I glare back at her, knowing my eyes reflect that.

"But I can't let them squash down a part of me," she tries a different tactic to get me on her side. Too bad for her that there isn't any part of me that wants this for her.

"Yes, you can. You are a Dragon," I say, going to take her hands. "You are the Dragon Empress. You did it, Little Dragon. Don't go looking for trouble when you are going to have enough to accomplish."

I see her defiance for another few seconds, but then her shoulders slump.

"Maybe," she pouts at me enticingly.

"Definitely," I insist, leading her over to the fireplace and lighting it with a little orb of Dragon fire.

The cozy glow brings her some comfort. I can see the tension leave her, so I play on it. I push her down to the rug and then start to massage her shoulders.

She groans with satisfaction.

"Dracul is awake?" I hesitantly ask.

"Yeah, he's fine. Still exactly the same, minus the Power to back him up."

We fall into an easy silence, and Delinda relaxes completely. I, however, am anything but relaxed. I am so fraught with this Fae thing; I am going to have to take this matter into my own hands. I must go and see Aefre and Remiel and tell them they have to bind the Fae powers in my wife immediately. She will only bring trouble to our door, that we do not need. I don't care if they have to do it without her consent. She will have this creature suppressed in her, or I will die trying. Because I am as sure as I sit here, I will die trying to protect her if this secret ever comes out.

As soon as Delinda falls asleep on the hearth, I scoop her up and put her on the bed next to Pres.

I reach over to To'Kah and shove him, not so gently, to wake him up. "Get up," I hiss at him.

He groans and opens his eyes to see me standing over him. "What is it?" he asks, sitting up suddenly.

"Shh," I hiss at him and then indicate with my hand that he should follow me.

I Astral outside and within seconds, he does the same, dressed and full of concern.

"We need to nip this in the bud," I say to him in a whisper. "We need to go to her parents and convince them they need to bind her Fae powers again."

"Let's go," he says briskly.

I knew he would be on board with this. I probably should wake Pres up and have him join us, but I leave him with Delinda. She will sleep more soundly with her husband next to her.

I nod at him and we head out on foot to find them.

Unexpectedly, we meet them coming up the stairs at the same time we are going down.

We all pause and look at each other for a second before we all blurt out, "We need to talk."

The tension drops slightly and Aefre grabs our hands. With Remiel gripping her elbow, she Astrals us outside, high up on the cliff tops where no one can overhear us, and Dracul is waiting for us, looking grim.

30

~TO'KAH~

*A*efre drops our hands the second that she can and starts to wring them in front of her, looking very unsure of herself for once.

"Where is Pres'Ton?" Dracul asks, glaring at us.

"He is sleeping with Delinda," Rex says, and then coughs as Aefre and Remiel shoot daggers at him. "I mean sleeping," he insists. "She will sleep better with her husband by her side. We will fill him in."

Dracul growls at us, not amused that we have left out Delinda's Beta husband. "We are here because we are all on the same page and we need to act. Now."

"I couldn't agree more," I grit out.

"Wait," Rex says suddenly.

He rubs his hand on the back of his head, also looking slightly unsure of himself now.

"Having a crisis of conscience?" I bark at him.

He fixes me with a fierce stare. "Actually, yes. She will never forgive us if we do this to her without her consent. The only thing I am concerned about is getting that Fae fucker out of her life. The rest, I can live with and die trying to protect her if I have to."

Aefre beams at him, and even Remiel gives him a nod of

approval. The jealousy that flares up in me is vicious. I will never be accepted that way by either of them. It never used to bother me. A few days ago, I couldn't care less if I ever saw either one of them again, but now? Now that Delinda and I are together and having a child, I need them to accept that, and me.

"*I* will die trying to protect her," I snap at him. "But we won't be put in that position if we can get rid of the Fae side." That's when what he actually said hits me. "What Fae fucker?" I add with a growing sense of panic.

He huffs at me. "Oh, uhm, Delinda told us about him after you left."

My heart thumps. "What did she say?"

"Only that he made a connection with her through her magick when she used it to transfer the Power. She doesn't know anything else."

"Why didn't anyone fill me in on this before?" I am beyond hurt that they all kept this from me.

"You stormed out, she came clean, we made up and then you came back and we..." he glances at Aefre and Remiel quickly, "...made up some more and fell asleep, then she fell asleep and now we are here."

"Humph," I mutter. "This just confirms to me that we have to squash this side of her. I will not let her get involved with them." I pin Aefre's eyes and she looks at me, the way she used to, for a brief moment, like she cares.

"I will not let this Empire be run by the Fae," Dracul suddenly roars into our faces, scaring us shitless.

"It won't be," Aefre snarls at him. "Delinda is still the same as she always was. She always had her Fae side. We just need to convince her not to use the powers, that's all."

"I thought you were in agreement that we had to bind her?" Dracul snarls back.

"I was!" she shouts. "But I have changed my mind. Rexus is right, she will never forgive us, and we are already in the fucking doghouse over the whole To'Kah thing!"

I blink at her. That 'To'Kah thing' was my almost-execution. So glad that she gives a shit, I think sarcastically.

Rex grabs my hand and squeezes it, knowing how hurtful that was. But then I remember that he is trying to keep Delinda's Fae side alive and drag my hand out of his. I fold my arms across my chest defensively.

"Delinda knows that was just a ploy," Dracul spits out and my eyes go wide.

"What?" I snap at him. "She knows?" Oh, the gods. She was never supposed to find out. I know what she must be thinking: that I was willing to abandon her just when we were starting our life together.

Shit.

Fuck.

She is going to kick my ass.

Dracul glares at me for yelling at him. "Yes, she knows. I told her to see if it would get her angry enough at me to do what needed to be done. Clearly, it didn't."

The dig is unmistakable. We all heard it. Aefre chokes back a noise that I hope isn't amusement. Rex is staring at me in shock. Yeah, going to have some explaining to do later. Right now, we need to solve this issue.

"So, what do we do?" I ask.

"We are at an impasse," Aefre says. "I won't bind her powers again."

"You have to," Remiel says. "This is the best thing for her."

"I agree," I pipe up, hoping to get on his good side.

I get a cursory glance, probably just so that he doesn't appear rude.

She looks at Dracul. "Only you know what this Power holds. Can she do this without the strength her Fae powers are giving her? Is she strong enough?"

We all look at Dracul now and hold our breath as we wait for his answer.

It takes a really long time.

"No," he states finally. "She isn't. She wasn't ready for this. We were pushed into this by a variety of outside factors, and now we have activated this Fae connection bullshit." He glares at Aefre. "You need to find out who it is."

"What difference will that make?" I exclaim.

"Every difference," Aefre replies. "If he is a low-level Fae, then we know that Delinda's powers are what called to him. If he is strong, then we know it was him seeking her out."

"How would he even know?"

Aefre sighs. "Now that I know what lengths everyone has gone to in order to get Delinda, I am absolutely sure that they did the same. They'll have taken her blood and cast a spell of some kind when she was little and living there. They will have chosen a mate for her the second they found out who she was."

"And who is she, exactly?" I ask. I seem to be the only one in the dark.

"The Blessed baby," Aefre says.

I groan. "You mean she is meant to rule there as well?"

"Kind of. She was meant to unite the Kingdoms. *Is* meant to unite the Kingdoms. Drake has another daughter, who they have pimped out already to a Light Fae to breed, but it was always Delinda".

"You have a Fae sister?" I ask, forgetting that I am supposed to speak only when spoken to, if that, around her and Remiel.

"Ugh," she spits out. "Ambrosia! Silly bitch."

I blink at her and her vehemence. Well, okay then. Best leave that hornet's nest alone.

"So, what are we doing?" Rex asks. "Vote?"

"No, there is no vote!" Dracul thunders. "We do what is best for the Empire."

"And what about what is best for Delinda?" I ask, wondering why I am not backing him up.

"The Empire comes first," he states.

"Not to me," I growl.

"Nor me," Rex says.

"You were for this a moment ago," Dracul accuses me.

I shrug. "Look, I hate that Delinda has a Fae side, I hate it even more that she now has this Fae fucker coming after her. I also hate that her Dragon has to be anywhere near that power. But it isn't up to me. Or you. Or any of us."

I came to this realization only a moment ago. I don't even know how. I came here determined to end this and now I don't want to. I want Delinda to be happy. I don't want her hating me, us, for what we did to her. It will make her bitter and resentful and any chance we had will go flying out of the window. I will lose her, Her and my child in one fell swoop. I will have to deal with the Fae thing on my own, in my own time. Delinda and my child are all that matters.

"I agree," Rex says, barely contributing to this conversation at all. I give him a frustrated look. "I *do* think finding out who this fucker is needs to be done. We need to know who we are up against."

I nod, as does Aefre.

Remiel is still glowering at us all. I get why, he doesn't want any reminder that Delinda isn't his.

"And we keep this secret beyond the grave," I state solemnly. "We all need to convince Delinda to keep the Fae powers under wraps. No one can know."

"And if she doesn't comply?" Dracul growls.

"Then we revisit."

"First with threats and then with action if that doesn't work," Aefre says. "If we stand united on this, she will have no choice but to listen to us. Dracul?"

He huffs out a breath. "Fine. But she gets one chance. *One*! If I see her using those powers, *I* will be the one to threaten her."

"Got it," Rex and I say in unison. We have our work cut out for us. We need to bring Pres in on this as soon as possible.

"Let us go to her first," Rex says. "When we have had the

145

discussion, we will fill you in and then you can back us up. Organically. Don't force it. She will rebel."

Aefre snorts in agreement, and elbows Remiel.

"Fine," he grumbles.

They Astral off and so does Dracul. We need to watch him. He caved in too easily. Then again, I suppose, I did too. Standing here, discussing Delinda like she meant nothing to us, and only that she is the Empress, wasn't right.

"Pres is going to kick our asses that we left him out," I say.

Rex chuckles. "He could try, but yeah. We need to fill him in and make this right."

I nod and we both Astral off the cliff top and back to our new Empress and her sleeping husband.

31

~PRES~

I'm jarred awake by a shove and a hand clapped over my mouth when my eyes pop open. I see Rex and To'Kah shushing me, but other than that, I don't sense any danger.

I peel Rex's hand from my mouth. "What?" I whisper.

"Just get dressed and come outside the Fortress," he whispers back and then they are gone.

I glance down at Delinda and she is still sound asleep, so I climb carefully off the bed, Astral my clothes on and then head outside.

I find Rex and To'Kah near the wall on the opposite side to our bedroom. "What is going on?" I ask striding forward, hands clenched.

"Dracul is flaming mad, and he has given Delinda one chance. We must convince her not to use her Fae powers under any circumstances, or he is going to, firstly threaten her with her life, and if he has to go back a second time, he will act. Now, he won't kill her, obviously, but he can make her suffer." Rex gives me a grim look.

"She is the Empress!" I blurt out. "He can't do that."

"Oh, he can," To'Kah growls. "We are all expendable and

don't think for a second he is above throwing any of us into that pit. *Again.*"

"Oh, yes, about that…" Rex snarls at him, but To'Kah puts his hand up.

"Another time, Rex."

"She will protect us," I say, but I know she can't watch us every second, and that is all it will take Dracul to get to one of us.

"Look, that is just one way he can get to her. There are a dozen others. She is not strong enough yet to enforce this power. *We* have to get her strong enough quickly and *without* the Fae side," Rex says urgently.

"Why can't we just bind her powers, like last time?" I ask with a frown.

"We agreed it wasn't an option. She would never forgive us," Rex says briskly, looking anywhere but at me.

"And who is 'we'?" I give them both a dirty look. Seems they have been plotting without me.

"It wasn't intentional," To'Kah says diplomatically. "We met her parents while we were talking and they Astralled us off. We felt it best that you stayed with Delinda so that she rested properly. If we had all gotten up and left her, she would have woken and come to find us. So, we need to move this along, before that exact thing happens now."

I let out a low rumble. He has a point, but still. It's unfair that they go off to plot, leaving me behind to babysit, not to mention, leaving me out of the decisions. "What if I don't agree?"

"You have no choice." Rex states.

"Don't I?" I challenge him, clenching my fists.

"Look, you can cast a spell to squash her Fae side, but you will be on your own, and when she finds out, you will be gone. It's up to you," To'Kah lays it on the line with force.

"Why did *you* change your mind? Hmm? You were the one who left her over this in the first place," I practically yell at him.

"I changed my mind," he says mildly. "I put her feelings first instead of my own, which is what this is all about."

Well, he has me there. She is my world, and I would do anything for her. I just don't want her lying to us and going behind our backs with any of this stuff. "If we try to convince her, how will we know if she sticks to it?"

They both sigh and run their hands through their hair. "We won't if she does it on the sly. But if we are there to remind her of the consequences, then hopefully it will be enough for her. We have the job of initial contact. Her parents will back us up, when the time is right."

"Oh, great," I grumble. "Put our lives on the line first."

Rex snorts. "We have a better chance of persuading her when she will be most amenable."

My cheeks go slightly warm at that thought. Ganging up on her during sex is a low move that we shouldn't be proud of, but we have no choice by the sounds of it. Dracul means business and while he may not be Emperor anymore, I *am* worried that Delinda is not strong enough yet. "We need to perform these spells today," I blurt out. "The sooner our lives are tied to one another, the safer we will all be."

"Agreed," they both mutter.

"I'll go and start the prep," I say, and Astral off before either one of them can say another word. They have done enough. Making decisions on my behalf is very shitty of them. It shows me what they think of me. That I am not important enough to be included.

I have worked myself up into a right temper by the time I enter my mother's old workshop. I start slamming stuff around, then I stop dead when I feel Delinda behind me. I turn to the door with a smile that freezes instantly.

"Pres," Aefre says to me. "Everything okay?"

"Yes," I croak out. The force of that connection I feel is on a par to what I feel around Delinda. Not good. I must break this Chosen bond. Now. "Just getting the spell together."

She nods at me. "You're doing this now?"

"Yes."

"Good. The stronger your connection to her, *all* of you, the more likely she is to agree to not using her Fae powers."

"Is that all?" I ask her, with way more courage than I would normally have, and that I pulled up from very deep inside me.

Her green eyes go slightly wide at my dismissal of her. "Guess so," she murmurs and Astrals off, leaving me anxious. I hope that I haven't pissed her off. Then I scowl. I shouldn't even care about that. Delinda is all that matters.

With that firmly in my mind, I set to work and within the hour, I have everything I need for the severing spell. Now to get to work on the tie-to-life one which is far more dangerous and complicated.

32

~DELINDA~

I stand in the shower, alone and quite enjoying it that way for a minute. Since the wedding, I have precious little time to myself. I adore my men and I am so grateful for them, even though I am still annoyed with To'Kah and his rash decisions of late. I will have to find the time to address these issues soon.

Not to mention, since I woke up, he and Rex have been like two hovering beasts. Fuck knows where Pres is. He has disappeared and I can't sense him. If he isn't back by the time I get out of the shower, I will go and search for him.

I run my hands down my wet body and stop at my stomach, putting my hand protectively over it. I know the baby is safe after that immense Power overload. She is a Dragon, and the Power is Dragon. I knew it wouldn't harm her.

I take a moment to assess myself in this rare moment of privacy. I haven't really had a chance to before now.

I feel very different. I feel the Power coursing through me. It makes me tired and hungry, but it's a small price to pay until I get used to it.

I smile to myself.

I did it!

I am the Empress of the Dragon Realms.

I let that sink in for a moment, before the nerves set in. We must move swiftly to let everyone know that *I* rule these Realms now.

I turn the shower off and climb out, wrapping a towel around myself and marching back into the bedroom.

I stop short when my declaration to arrange a coronation is put on hold by my three men, looking at me in varying degrees of fright.

"What?" I ask immediately. "What's happened?"

"Err, nothing," Rex stammers, but he is a shit liar.

I fix him with my best stern look, and he withers slightly, which makes me think whatever he has to say is pretty bad.

"We have something to discuss," To'Kah says.

I narrow my eyes at him. "Oh, yes, we do," I drawl. "I know about your and my uncle's diabolical plan."

He looks sheepish but shakes his head. "We will get to that. Right now, we need to cast a couple of spells."

Rex and Pres give him filthy looks.

"What kind of spells?" I ask, fully aware that they hate my Fae powers and if they are even thinking about binding them, I will smite them all where they stand. Okay, not really, but I like the danger that I can back up that threat, nonetheless.

Pres takes over, approaching me with caution. "The first one is a severing spell..."

"OH, I DON'T THINK SO!" I roar at him, making him stumble back from the sheer volume of it. "You come anywhere near me with a Fae powers severing spell and I will end you!"

"It's not for that," he bleats. "Hear me out?"

I like that he posed that as a question, so I nod regally and allow him to continue.

I know I am acting quite bitchy, but I have suddenly gone very protective of my Fae powers. They got me what I wanted without having to murder my uncle. I don't get why everyone thinks this is a bad thing.

"It's a severing spell that will effectively get rid of the

Chosen bond that you have with me and Rex, as well as Trey and their father."

He stops speaking, waiting for me to react.

I clench my jaw and think over what he just said. Yes, I agree that Trey and Septimus have to go, but Rex and Pres? I give them a frown.

"I don't like that idea. I don't want to lose this bond that I have with you."

They both give me a big beaming smile, but it doesn't last long.

Pres clears his throat and carries on, "We are then going to create a tie-to-life spell, the same one that your mother has with her husbands. That will tie the four of us together, with you as the anchor."

"Oh," I say, relieved that they weren't trying to get rid of the bond for good, just to create a new one. "One that will exclude everyone else." I nod firmly.

"And *include* To'Kah," Rex points out.

"Yes, I like it. How do we do it?"

I get three relieved looks, and shaky smiles. They really thought that I wouldn't go for this? That is a bit of a reality check. I bite the inside of my cheek. I have been acting like a raving bitch lately. I don't mean to. I would like to blame it on pregnancy hormones, but that is just a cop out. I need to make it up to them. They looked petrified of me earlier and that won't do. They are my loves, my life. We are equal in this relationship. My Empress status is separate from this. I have to make this up to them. Make them see that I love them, and I want what is right for all of us. An idea starts to form, and it is out of my mouth before I can really think it through.

"I know that you are all worried about my Fae powers, but you needn't be. I know that I can't use them here. At least not until I have tried to build bridges with them, and you must understand, I must *try*. We are both the original creatures, Dragons and Fae, we should be living in harmony, not animosity. I can change the perspective over time, but until then, rest assured, I will not use these powers."

The looks, and rush of feelings, I get from the three men makes me know, without a doubt, that I have made the right decision.

"Oh, Delly," Pres cries, dropping to his knees in front of me and grabbing my hand. "You are just perfect."

Rex and To'Kah do the same, with similar words on their lips and I preen with the compliments and love.

"Now, how do we do these spells?" I ask. "Are they safe for the baby?"

"It's completely safe," Pres informs me, getting to his feet. "A little tricky, especially timing wise, but I will complete the severing spell after Rex starts the tie-to-life spell. I must warn you that it contains a lot of Black magick, but the Blood magick rules the spell despite that, okay?"

"Yes, I'm aware." I remember mother doing this spell with her husbands.

He nods at me. "If you are, at any point, worried about the baby, tell me and we will stop."

I give him a soft look, that he returns. "You are precious," I say and give him a kiss. He, *they* are willing to risk breaking the Chosen connection and not completing the tie-to-life spell for the safety of our baby. It makes me realize that this is true between us. Bonds aside, these three men are mine and we don't need the magick behind us to be in love and to make this relationship work. *We* are all the magick we need. "I love you all. Now where do you want me?"

I roll my eyes at the lusty looks I get, but I suppose I did walk into that one, standing just in a towel. In a quick swirl, I am dried, dressed and ready for action. "Oh, and when we are done here, we need to plan a coronation."

"Your mother is already on top of that," Pres says quickly, avoiding my gaze. What is he hiding?

I add that to the growing list of issues that need dealing with. It can all wait until after these spells are complete.

Pres arranges a bunch of candles around and places me at the pinnacle, with Rex and To'Kah on either side of me, our hands linked. Pres stands in front of me and lights the candles with his mind, which impresses me.

"I'm sorry," he whispers, before he takes a wickedly sharp athame and drags it across each of my wrists.

I hiss at the pain and watch as he does the same to Rex and then himself.

He starts to chant a spell in Dragon; a language in which I am not as fluent as I would like to be. Again, this needs to be rectified immediately. How can I rule these Realms and not know the language inside and out?

I gasp as I feel the life draining out of me and grip Rex's hand tighter as he stumbles. I give Pres a horrified look, but he shakes his head with determination and carries on. I have to trust him.

Rex drops to his knees, his head bowed as he writhes in pain. I think I am only still on my feet due to my Power. This spell is vicious.

A wave of nausea goes over me and I close my eyes, feeling the breeze whipping my hair around. I can feel my connection to the two men I am bound to, flitting away, filling me with a dread that I have never felt. It is the dread of losing the ones that you love the most, the ones that are your life, your heart.

"No!" I scream. "Stop! Please! I can't lose you!"

"Let them continue," To'Kah presses. "You can do this."

I pant, opening my eyes to look at him. He is solid and reassuring next to me, so I trust him.

"Keep going," he says to Pres.

Pres nods determinedly. He starts to chant quicker and more forcefully.

"Rex?" To'Kah shouts at him over the deafening roar of the vortex and Pres's cries. "Can you do this?"

Rex grips my hand tighter, hauling himself to his feet. "Yes," he croaks out.

Pres nods and without missing a beat, slashes To'Kah across the wrists and then Rex starts to chant in Latin.

"Aah!" I cry out as the swirling mess of the different magicks rush through me, out of me, coiling around me, entering my mouth, up my nose, through my eyes. I shriek with sheer terror as I am, *we are*, completely enveloped in a black and red cloud of pure power.

I feel Pres's hands on my wrists, gripping tightly as he takes over the tie-to-life spell from Rex. His hold on me is strong. I breathe out in relief, knowing that this is going the way it is supposed to. He knows what he is doing; he is confident and that relaxes me. I fall into a bit of a stupor as the words and magick wash over me and then it is quiet.

Too quiet. "Are you okay?" I blurt out, still shrouded in a thick fog that impairs my vision.

"Yes," come back three voices. "Are you? The baby?"

"Just fine," I laugh nervously and drag my hands out of theirs so that I can wave them in front of my face to clear the fog. I cough and so do they and then we can see each other. They are beaming at me, clearly feeling the effects of the spell. I feel all wiggly inside. Like the different magicks are fighting for pride of place.

I am not happy about this, Princess.

I blink at the rage I hear in his voice in my head. But push it aside. Who cares what he thinks? I don't even know him. All that matters are the three men in front of me and the force of my love for them.

"We did it!" Pres breathes, elated.

"*You* did it," Rex says, the pride in his voice making the tears spring to my eyes. "Good job, kid."

Pres laughs, his hand on his chest. "Wow. This is so much more."

"I know," I laugh back at him, full of joy at these feelings that have settled on me like they belong. "And you..." I look at To'Kah. I have never had a bond to him as such. He is bonded with my Dragon, of course, but this is so far beyond that now.

He drops his forehead to mine, his eyes closed. "I love you," he murmurs.

I take his face in my hands and give him a sweet kiss as Rex presses his lips to the nape of my neck and Pres places his hand on the small of my back.

"One," he whispers. "One."

33

~REX~

I am fucked. I can barely stand up, but I seem to be the only one that has been affected so badly by these two spells. I know it was the severing spell that kicked my ass. Pres seemed to be just fine. Maybe because my connection was real and needed to dig deeper than his.

Delinda smiles at me and leads me to the rug in front of the fireplace, pushing me down and straddling me. I honestly don't think, in all of my thousand plus years, I have ever turned down a jump before, but I don't think I can right now.

"You okay?" she murmurs to me, her lips on mine.

I close my eyes and fall even more in love with her. She knows the spell took it out of me, but she also knows that I don't want the other two men to know how weak I am right now.

"Yes," I murmur back, my hands on her hips, "but this is going to have to wait."

She just nods as To'Kah and Pres seat themselves next to us.

"I need to speak to my mother about this coronation," she declares, standing up.

I see the disappointment flash on the faces of the two men.

They were hoping for some action, but I give her a grateful smile.

"Yes, go, Little Dragon, and then when you get back, we can take this bond for a test drive."

She snorts in amusement as Pres gives me a weird look, then she Astrals off.

"What's a test drive?" Pres asks.

I chuckle. "It's an Earth thing. You really need to go sometime. But don't worry about it. Right now, I want to talk about what Delinda said before we cast the spells. Do we trust her?"

"Yes," To'Kah says. "We must. She has made her intentions known that she's trying to build bridges, and it is our duty to support her."

"Agreed," Pres says.

I nod slowly. I heard the voice in her head earlier. I wasn't sure if the others did, which is why I was coy about bringing this up. It is clear that they didn't. I wonder why I did. Is it because I had a real connection to her in the first place? Either way, this Fae fucker is not happy about the bond we have formed, and I am sure it won't be the last we hear from him.

Asshole. I hope that one day I can get my hands on him and beat him to death for daring to stake a claim on my wife.

"I need to say something," To'Kah croaks out after a lengthy pause. "I need you two to back me up."

"What is it?" I urge, sitting up straight.

"I am going to ask Delinda to marry me. As soon as possible. I just need you two to tell her it's a good idea and that we should do it."

I stifle my snort, as it isn't funny, poor guy, but I have never seen him so vulnerable before. It stirs my cock in a way that makes me uncomfortable. I promised Delinda that we wouldn't engage without her. Not to mention, I am suddenly feeling a hundred percent and as horny as fuck.

Where is she?

My sudden desperation makes the other two men frown at me.

"You don't want this?" To'Kah barks at me.

"What? No. Don't be ridiculous. I want my wife to return. But, yes, of course we will back you up. We need to make this official. Even more so because of the baby."

"My thoughts exactly," Pres says, looking around. "Where is she?" he adds desperately, echoing my thought.

Oh, shit. The implications of what we have just done, hit me. They can feel everything I can and vice versa. There must be a way to control that. I think I need to head to Earth and talk to Aefre's husbands about this.

Err, where did that thought come from?

My face goes thunderous as I look at Pres. That was *his* feeling about this, not mine. "Are you still harboring feelings for her?" I bark at him.

"What? Who?"

"Good question," To'Kah growls. "I don't like this. How do we control it?"

"Exactly why I was thinking we should go to the men who are in the same situation," Pres says, flustered. "Nothing more. I swear it."

"Humph," I say rudely. "Back to the marriage. You ask her and we will back you up. Now, if you will excuse me. I need to get away from you two for a bit. You are messing with my head."

"Same," they say and get up to leave just as I do.

I head to the shower and turn it on as hot as I can stand it. I must make sure that Pres and To'Kah don't find out about my knowledge of this Fae fucker and that he is firmly embedded in Delinda's mind. I don't even want Delinda to know I know. Not yet. I must find out who it is and Aefre said she could do that. I must go and speak to her about this as soon as she is finished with Delinda.

With that resolved, I let the water cascade over me and enjoy the peace and quiet in my head while I can. I get the feeling it is going to be sometime before we get a handle on this.

34

~DELINDA~

Two days later, I'm being prepped to take my rightful place as Empress of the Dragon Realms and Underworld. That last bit is an add-on. It's only because Tiamat created the Underworld. I don't think I actually rule there. The different species have their own leaders. Most of whom are, or were, involved with my mother at one point or another.

I have been working furiously with Uncle D behind the scenes for the last two days. He has given me a crash course in running this Empire. I am exhausted. I intend on delegating most of this out — I have no idea why he didn't — but to whom, remains to be seen. I guess I will have to start interviewing candidates soon. I want to be available when my child is born, not tucked away in an office doing mundane paperwork.

"Tighter," Synthyia grunts at me, her foot on my ass as she tugs on this black, lace corset with all the strength of an... well, an ancient Dragon.

I gasp as all the air is shoved out of me, while Mother snickers in the corner, all nice and comfy in her loose-fitting gown.

I should be the one in the loose-fitting gown, being pregnant and all. This poor child is currently being squashed for the sake of Dragon Empress propriety.

"I am *so* glad corset days are over," she says, still chuckling at me. "Those were the pits."

"You don't say," I manage to wheeze out.

Synthyia tugs again, but enough is enough.

"Please stop," I beg her. "I'm pregnant, remember. Get me a gown like hers." I gesture to my mother.

We all stop dead for just a moment in time, then my and Synthyia's eyes go straight to Mother's belly.

"What?" I shriek, pulling away from Synthyia, making her stumble as she still had her foot on my backside and a hold of the corset laces. "Are you pregnant as well? Is it Papa's?" The joy I feel is smooshed when she shakes her head.

"Oh," I state with a pout.

"I *am* pregnant," she clarifies quietly. "But it's Devon's."

My eyes go wide. "Ooh," I say with a smile. "Oh, that's wonderful." I didn't think it was possible between them, but they found a way obviously. "What did your other husbands think of that? What does *Papa* think of that?"

"They don't know yet. Unless Dev has opened his big, fat mouth about it while I've been here," she grumbles goodnaturedly. "As for your father, he knows and accepts it. He has no choice."

I snicker. She has such a way with her men. I love how she interacts with each of them and I count on that one day, I can have relationships like that with my men. So far, it has been a whirlwind and I haven't had time to process much of what has happened yet.

"Your Highness, please," Synthyia says, "we really don't have much time left."

"Fine, but ease up on the tugging," I complain, glad that this little interlude has given the laces a chance to loosen.

"As you wish," she murmurs and, with a bit more thought as to my unborn baby, laces up the corset with very little tightening.

She sighs in disappointment but turns me around and tells me how beautiful I look, anyway.

Mother grabs Synthyia by the hand and puts her finger to her lips. "Remember, no one else knows yet."

Synthyia nods. "I won't utter a word until the Empress makes the announcement."

Mother lets her go and she scampers off. I frown after her.

"What is it?" Mother asks.

"When *are* we going to announce I'm pregnant?" I ask, even though that is a question she can't answer. "I mean To'Kah and I need to do this soon."

"Coronation first, that can come afterwards. It is a good order. Cement your reign and then inform your subjects you have an heir." She pauses and frowns at me.

"What is it?" I ask her now.

"Do you plan on marrying him?" she asks delicately.

"Yes, of course. I was going to ask him after the ceremony today."

"*You* are going to ask *him*?" she splutters.

I roll my eyes at her. "Yes, Mother. This isn't the Middle Ages. I can ask a man to marry me."

"Humph," she says. "He should have the balls to ask you first."

"I think he wanted to, after the tie-to-life spell, but things have gone a bit pear-shaped with that."

"How so?"

"We feel each other's feelings, *all* of the time. We can't stand to be around each other much, and we haven't even had sex in two days!" I shriek, frustrated and upset.

"What?" she blurts out. "What are you doing?"

"Nothing. I don't think. Pres says it all went according to plan, but if he feels insecure about something, Rex and To'Kah do as well. If I'm feeling nauseous, all three of them are green as well. It's…it's…" I burst out crying as I have no words.

Mother gathers me to her and gives me a cuddle, then

pushes me away. "That's how it is supposed to be, but you have to work through it. Try to control what goes through the bond and what doesn't. It takes practice and some mental blocks, but you will figure it out together. You cannot keep avoiding each other, it's ridiculous."

"I know," I snivel into the tissue I magicked up. "I feel even closer to all of them and I haven't been able to express that because we keep driving each other away with our worst feelings about stuff. I'm over it. I want things back the way they were."

"Well, that isn't going to happen," she says with a sigh. "So, you can only move forward."

I nod. I know she is right, and I've hated to admit this, but feel better about it. We have to pull together and get through the first bits. We can figure it out as we go.

"Now, get yourself right, we don't have much more time."

"I'm ready," I say, fluffing out my hair. Mother puts the True Heir crown on my head that I wore for my wedding, which will be replaced by my Empress crown when I am sworn in.

The nerves hit me suddenly and I gulp. This gathering is going to be even bigger than the wedding, and that was pretty huge. I will be standing up there all on my own, probably driving my men nuts with my nerves as well.

"You have nothing to be scared of," Mother whispers to me. "This is your destiny."

I give her a shaky smile and then it is time to go.

She leads me out of the room, my black gown swishing around my ankles. The lace on the sleeves is a bit scratchy on my sensitive skin. I think that is a pregnancy symptom. Stuff like this never used to bother me before. Or maybe it's my nerves. I am acutely aware of absolutely everything as we descend the stairs. I am grateful Mother gave me this time to get myself together, instead of just Astralling me outside the Great Hall.

She tugs on my hand as I stop dead, planting my feet.

"Come," she says.

I shake my head. I can feel the anxiety from my men out here. If I go in there, it will send us all into a meltdown.

"You have to," she chides me. "You can't be sworn in outside in the ante-chamber."

"Why not?"

She rolls her eyes at me. "Because you can't," she states and that is apparently the end of that, as she has folded her arms across her chest and is giving me the evil eye.

"Fine," I grumble.

"And calm down, will you? I can see the 'FH'."

"What? What code is that?" I ask perplexed.

"Fae Heritage," she whisper-snaps at me.

I look above me, and yep, there it is. The white and gold light bouncing around.

"Shit," I mumble and try to calm my nerves. "You are going to have to go in there and ask them to leave," I add desperately.

"Who?"

"My men! They are doing this to me."

"Oh," she says, understanding dawning. "Wait here. I'll go and talk to them."

She stalks off, through the doors, where apparently everyone was waiting for me to make my entrance and are bitterly, and vocally, disappointed to see only my mother.

"Fuck," I whisper, wringing my hands.

After about a minute has passed, she returns, and I feel a calm wash over me.

"You did it," I sigh in relief. "What did you say to them?"

"Never mind that, now get moving!" She lightly slaps my ass to get me walking forward.

I hesitantly take a step forward, the biggest moment of my life upon me. Everything that I am has led to this one moment, and it is fucking terrifying. The Power transfer was nothing. That was easy, but this is…I gulp when I step into the Great Hall and over a thousand Dragons, in human form, all turn to look at me.

There is a hushed silence as I make my approach to Uncle D, who is standing right at the far end, with Papa on his other side, beaming. That breaks my tension. I don't think I have ever seen him 'beam' before. It looks so weird on his face that I have to bite my lip to stop the nervous hilarity that is about to break free.

Every person drops to their knees as I walk past row after row, crammed with my subjects. My skyscraper heels are the only sound in the Hall, clacking on the stone floor.

Mother insisted on these to make me appear taller. I am not that short, not next to her anyway, but in a room full of pure-blood Dragons, I am tiny. I am glad that she made me slip these on.

I finally reach the top of the Hall, seeing my men in the front row, on their knees, their heads bowed in reverence, until I pass and then they stand to usher me the final few steps to Uncle Dracul.

Mother's doing, obviously, as this was supposed to be a solo event. It has calmed us all down.

Uncle D is giving me a look of such pride that I simper slightly, then adjust my features as Rex elbows me gently with a soft snort of amusement.

I get no feelings of anxiety from them, just lots of support and it gets me through the next stomach-clenching minute.

The men shuffle themselves around so that I am facing the crowd now. The huge golden throne, that was partially hidden behind the massive frame of Uncle D, comes into view and I stare at it. I don't know where it came from. I haven't seen it before. Uncle D never went in for all that pomp and ceremony. I wonder if I should or try to be more approachable.

"Sit," Uncle D whispers to me, grabbing my hand and helping me move forward towards the throne.

Mother has joined Papa now and catches my eye, rolling hers to the ceiling. I stifle my chuckle by biting my tongue. Hard. Then they are all on their knees in front of me again.

Except Mother.

It reminds me then that she is Queen here. She kneels for no one, not even me. She stands at my side, her hand resting lightly on the back of the throne.

"Empress," Uncle D says lifting his head, his lips trying not to smirk at me. "Do you vow to rule and protect this Empire with everything that you have until the time comes to pass your rule onto your heir?"

"Yes," I croak out, expecting a whole lot more to come, but that's it. Apparently, it's enough to make it official, as he rises and takes the True Heir crown off my head and replaces it with a simple gold circlet that is way more my style than the gaudy opulence of the other one. Then he hands me a golden scepter with a flaming red crystal on the top and the Dragon-Slayer's sword.

The room collectively takes a nervous breath, but I smile and accept it, propping it up against the throne, tip down in a, hopefully, non-threatening way.

"Thanks," I mutter which makes my men glare at me wide-eyed. I'm guessing I'm supposed to say more. I open my mouth to attempt to say something appropriate, but Uncle D shakes his head imperceptibly. Okay, so I'm not supposed to say anything. This is confusing.

He then turns to the crowds and proceeds to give them a whole list of instructions and what they are, and aren't, supposed to do. This monologue is conducted in Dragon, so I tune out after a while, having lost the plot entirely. Mother must do the same as her hand lands on my shoulder. I look up at her and she is glaring at me ferociously.

I blink and gather my 'FH' is showing again. I give her a

stricken look, not daring to look at my men, but the rush of feelings I get, make it clear that they can see it as well.

I start to panic, which only makes it worse. If I am outed as half Fae *now* of all times, there will be a coup that even my parents won't be able to stop.

35

~TO'KAH~

I am frozen to the spot. Delinda has that white and gold glow about her that signifies her Fae side rearing its head. I am about to step forward and do damage control when her father does it for me.

He grabs her hand, and to my utter shock, digs his claws into her palm.

She hisses with the pain and her arm goes limp, but it does the job. The lights go out as she glares at him, but with understanding on her face.

I know that had to hurt her, but her arm is still slack like it has gone numb. I am guessing Remiel's claws are an upgraded version of regular Vampires, being what he is.

"Sorry," he mouths to her and she grimaces at him and looks away to see if anyone else had noticed. If they did, we won't know until they vocalize it, because as it appears, everyone is engrossed in Dracul's speech.

He gestures to her to stand up, and she does, shaking her arm out. She gives her best, winning smile. I am mesmerized by how it lights up her eyes. She is utterly gorgeous. If I hadn't already fallen in love with her, I would have now. I cast my glance across the crowd, and it appears that this is now the case with more than a handful of male Dragons that I can see. They are practically drooling over their new Empress. It's easy for them now. The threat of the Emperor was enough to keep everyone away from her in the past. Except me, of course, but that's different. Now, she can be admired openly; gawked and even leered at.

I hear Remiel growl low in his throat as he, too, spots the looks being cast upon his daughter.

I shuffle closer to her, at the exact same time as Rex and Pres do. I grimace at them, as they do at me.

This is an utter disaster.

Aefre threatened us with the fire pit if we didn't get over our nerves and start supporting our new Empress, telling us we had better get our asses up the second she passes us to join her and have her back.

We have been so separate from each other for the last two days; I didn't even get a chance to ask her to marry me. I must rectify that as soon as this is over. We have to start to figure out how to control this bond instead of having *it* control *us*.

I look over at Delinda and she is gazing lovingly at me. She knows what I am feeling about her right now and that's a good thing. This has its advantages, now we just need to figure out how to use it correctly. Maybe Rex's, or rather, *Pres's* idea of going to see Aefre's husbands isn't such a bad one. Although, I am sure Constantine would rather see anyone but me. Just another man that got wildly jealous that I was her Guardian.

Dracul looks over at Delinda and gives a slight tilt to his head.

She looks back at him blankly.

"Dismiss them," he whispers.

"Shouldn't I say something first?" she whispers back.

"Not today. That's for tomorrow."

"Oh." She clears her throat and then, with a voice as clear as a bell, she states, "Dismissed."

Everyone starts to file out, and she grabs my hand and

squeezes it. I lean down, about to drop a chaste kiss on her forehead, but before I can, she says, "Marry me."

I blink at her, surprised by her words. "That's my line," I say to her with a slight smile. She got to it before I could, because I am an utter dick and let this complication get in the way of what needs to be done.

She grins at me, but I have to do this right. I know that I should have done this in the first place. I let go of her and turn to her parents, dragging up every ounce of courage that I can, to face them and ask this most important question. Aefre cocks her eyebrow at me, knowing what is coming and moves closer to Remiel. I force myself to look into his ice-cold eyes and then back to Aefre as I say, "Your Highness, Remiel, I have loved your daughter for a very long time. I am dedicated to her and to her Dragon. I will spend every day making sure she knows how much I care about her. I will support her and give her everything that she needs to keep her and our child, happy. It would mean everything to me if you would give your permission for me to marry your daughter?"

"No," Remiel says instantly, with a look so ferocious, I am sure he is about to attack, but Aefre slaps her hand to his chest with a look that makes him stand down slightly.

"Yes," she says, looking back at me. "Our grandchild is more important to us now than whatever issues we have between us. We will put those aside to see you do right by our daughter and your child."

I breathe out in relief, even though Remiel clearly doesn't agree with her. But she will talk him around. She has offered up something that I would be a fool to refuse: a chance to ask her forgiveness.

"I'm sorry," I whisper to her, knowing that she will know what for.

She nods stiffly but says nothing. That's fine. I know that she has accepted it.

I nod back and then turn to Delinda. She is waiting with bated breath.

But I have one more thing to do first. I look at Rex and Pres. "Will you allow me to ask your wife to marry me?"

They both smirk at me and nod eagerly.

With a big grin, I drop to one knee and take her hand. "Delinda, will you do me the honor of becoming my wife?"

"Yes!" she screams in my face, dragging me up and capturing my mouth with hers for a deep kiss. "Yes! I will!"

I let out the breath I was holding and pull away from her, aware that her parents and uncle are glaring at this display.

"Tomorrow," she says. "We have to do this tomorrow and then we can announce that the heir has been conceived."

"Ahem," Dracul coughs, drawing our focus to him. "You cannot get married tomorrow and then tell the Empire you are pregnant. They will not accept that the child is *his*," he glares at me, "they will assume it belongs to one of your current husbands. You will wait."

Delinda frowns at him. "That makes no sense. I'm already two months along. They will know when the baby appears early."

"Not necessarily," Aefre says very quietly. "Your pregnancy will probably advance quickly like mine and Arathia's. If we keep that quiet, you can get away with making this official as is expected."

As one, we all glance out across the Great Hall. There are a few stragglers, those who probably caught my proposal and lingered to see what would happen.

They are at the back of the Hall, so probably didn't hear.

We all tear our eyes away, Delinda's going to mine. "Are you okay with waiting?" she asks anxiously.

"Yes," I say straight away. I will wait until the day the baby is born as long as we tell everyone the child is *mine*. If they had suggested passing it off as Rex or Pres's, it would've killed me.

She gives me a shaky smile. I know she isn't happy about

this, but I don't care about waiting. I just need to be with her and raise our child together, and in the future, have another pure-blood Dragon that I can pass my legacy onto. I know that this child, as the first-born, regardless that it will be born human, will rule. That means any other children we have will be free to train as Guardians.

"I love you," she whispers to me, then grabs Pres's and Rex's hands drawing them closer. "I think it is time we started using this bond properly. We cannot let our insecurities and negative feelings rule us."

"Yes," Rex says, more relaxed than I have seen him since we created the bond. "We will get through this. Together."

She nods with tears in her eyes, the beautiful smile on her face an image I will treasure for eternity.

36

~DELINDA~

I excuse us and Astral the four of us back to our bedroom. We need to power through this nightmare and move on. I try that mental blocks thing that Mother spoke of, trying to picture my thoughts and feelings being behind a wall. It seems to work as the men relax a smidge and then regard me curiously.

"Mental blocks," I say. "Perhaps you can try it?"

I watch them as they squint and scrunch up their faces, hiding my smile as they attempt to erect some kind of block against all of these swirling, messy feelings.

"Fantastic," Rex sighs. "I guess it will take some getting used to, holding them up all the time. Sleeping will be a problem."

"We will have to work on ignoring them," I say and then strip off my clothes. I am done worrying about this, and I am done waiting for my men to ravage me.

It works for them, as they strip off theirs just as quickly and approach me hungrily. Feeling naughty, I take a few steps back to the bed, keeping out of their reach for a few moments, until I fall back and let them crawl over to me.

I admire them for a brief moment. So very different to

each other in looks and attitude, but all so gorgeous it makes me lick my lips. My action causes them to growl at me and dive, pinning me to the bed as Rex and To'Kah land on either side of me, Pres on top of me, his cock already at attention.

"You ready for this, Little Dragon?" Rex whispers to me, before he drags me up and clamps down on my neck, biting me hard enough to make me squeal with the pain.

"Ahh!" I cry out as Pres impales me on his cock, forgetting all about foreplay. We are straight down to business after our forced hiatus, but I don't care. I want this. I want all of this.

Rex loosens his hold and kisses me gently where he bit down, before he trails his tongue all the way to my wrist as To'Kah leans in to suck my nipple into his mouth.

I squirm with ecstasy, my eyes squeezed shut, wishing that they would hurt me a little bit more. One more vicious bite, a scrape of talons across my sensitive skin, a gentle orb of Dragon fire bounced across my breasts, just enough to feel the burn.

Then it stops.

I open my eyes to find them looking at me with such love, I nearly weep.

"One day, my love," To'Kah whispers to me, "But not while you are pregnant. We can't risk hurting you or the baby, right now."

I sigh. I am so much stronger than they give me credit for. However, I have to love them for being so caring and concerned.

"Then fuck me as if there is no tomorrow, all ends, I want it all," I whisper and close my eyes again, succumbing to their raw desires. A pure driven lust that drives me over the edge again and again as all three of my holes are filled up simultaneously with cocks so engorged, I will feel them for a week.

I have lost count of the number of orgasms I've had. I have lost track of who is in which hole. All I know is that I am even more deeply in love with every single one of them and that the voice in my head is getting angrier and angrier as he shouts at me to dismiss them and have only him.

We belong together. We are the same. Lose them before you lose me.

"No," I moan in between my lovers switching places, before a cock is shoved into my mouth and a hand goes around my throat, tightly as if to prove a point.

My eyes pop open and I see Rex's furious eyes for a split second before the anger dissipates, and he floods my mouth with his cum so suddenly, I almost choke on it.

"You are *ours*," he growls at me, his hand tightening momentarily. "Stop thinking about him."

I can't help the shudder that goes through me as To'Kah makes me climax. How did Rex know that I was thinking about my Fae mate?

Pres stills underneath me, his huge cock in my ass as To'Kah continues to pound my pussy, unable to stop he is that close to his orgasm.

"Yours," I croak out, needing to say it, meaning it with everything that I have. I can't help his voice in my head. I don't really want it there. I made a decision and I intend to stick to it. "I love you!" I cry out before Rex crushes his mouth to mine in a savage kiss that makes me shiver with delight and longing for more.

Pres starts to move again, holding my hips in place as he thrusts higher and higher into my ass, before he roars his way through a climax that goes on and on.

I tremble one last time, coming fiercely before I fall under the spell of the three men, making love to me gently, taking turns instead of all at once.

I am almost asleep when Rex floods my body with his seed, withdrawing quickly from my pussy to croon to me.

I am exhausted.

The Power transfer has taken its toll on me, as is the actual Power. I have a big day tomorrow, addressing my subjects for the first time as their Empress. I am nervous and excited at the same time.

I smile, drifting off as my lovers clean me up, but I'm fast asleep before they are done with me.

I'm jolted out of my sleep by someone climbing over me to get off the bed.

"What?" I mumble, my eyes so heavy I don't want to open them, but I have to find out what is going on.

"Go back to sleep, Princess," Rex murmurs to me. "I will be back soon."

"Where are you going?" I ask, rubbing my eyes. "Give me a minute; I'll come with you."

"No, you stay here and sleep, my love. I won't be long."

Why is he being so evasive?

I sit up and force my eyes fully open so that I can scowl at him. "Where are you going?" I demand.

He sighs. "To see my father and brother. I want to make absolutely sure the Chosen bond has been severed with them. We were relying on my blood being enough seeing as they weren't here. I have to make sure."

He looks so worried about it, that I let him off the hook. I must be honest; it never even occurred to me. I just assumed they were gone from my life and that was it. I think this whole Fae thing has thrown me for a loop, as he is all I can think about with regard to men other than my lovers. Something that has to stop right now.

Never, Princess. I will always be here.

Dammit! He has *got* to go!

"What?" Rex asks me, narrowing his molten chocolate eyes at me. "What's wrong?"

"Nothing," I lie.

177

He huffs at me. I have a horrible feeling he knows more than he is letting on and that is very worrying. "Go back to sleep. I will kiss you awake when I return."

I nod numbly. I am so tired. I don't really want to go with him to see his father and brother, yet I feel like I need his reassurance. I want to remain in his presence for a little while longer so that I know he is okay, and that he doesn't know that I still have my Fae mate talking to me in my head.

"I love you so much, you know," I say earnestly. "I hope that you are happy?"

His shocked look makes me gulp. Have I made a grave error? Now he is going to know for sure that something is wrong,

He drops back down next to me, taking me in his arms. "Oh, Delinda," he sighs. "I have never known happiness like this before. I adore you. You are truly the love of my life. I never want to be away from you. But I have to do this. Okay?"

I nod. He seems to think that I am worried about him leaving to see his family. I have to let him think that because the alternative will hurt him too much. Hurt all of them far too much.

"Don't be long," I murmur and kiss him quickly.

"I won't," he says, pushing me gently back to the bed. "Sleep. I have things I want to do to you when I get back that require you to be awake."

I shiver at his delicious tone and give him a sleepy smile. "Kiss me awake when you get back and then do what you will to me."

His eyes darken as I give him my permission to ravage the shit out of me. But then they cloud over as he strokes my belly. "Soon," he mutters. "I want you in Dragon form. Soon."

My heart thumps. I want him that way too. All of them. It has never been an issue for me before. I have never wanted it. It seemed like hard work, and I am all for an easy life. But now, I can't wait to Shift for them and mate in our true forms.

"Yes," I whisper and give him something to think about as he nods and Astrals out of the bedroom, leaving me to contemplate that as well, and then finally drift off with the voice of my Fae mate in my head.

Never, Princess. You will never have them that way.

37

~REX~

I lied to Delinda.

I feel shit about it, but I was hoping to sneak off and be back before she woke up. Yes, I am going to see my father and Trey, but I have a stop to make first. I am growing more and more concerned about this Fae fucker. I can hear everything he is saying to her, and it is bothering me in ways that I never thought possible. I also know she is trying to ignore him, however, she is doing nothing to push him out.

I knock loudly on the door I landed in front of and wait.

Remiel opens the door with a suspicious look. "What?" he snaps at me.

"Is Aefre here?" I ask briskly, ignoring his menace in favor of my quest to get answers.

"She is away at the moment," he states and slams the door in my face.

"Great," I grumble and turn to leave.

But not a second later, the door flies open again and Aefre is standing there with an annoyed look on her face. "I just got back," she says. "What is it?"

I look to the left and right and then say, "May I come in?"

She steps back and allows me entry, shutting the door behind me.

"Can you find out who this Fae asshole is that has staked his claim on Delinda?" I ask, getting straight to the point.

"Yes," she nods. "In fact, I already know. I have just come from the Dark Fae Kingdom and Drake has filled me in. Rest assured, Delinda won't be going anywhere on my watch, as they have amped up their efforts now that Blayne has made contact with her. She won't be safe out of the Dragon Realms."

"Blayne?" I croak out. I know that name.

She nods. "He is a very powerful Light Fae. I never met him, I don't think, while I was spelled up to be with Sebastian. But he has off-the-charts powers, apparently. He is the son of Melisandre, Pyleah's half-sister."

"Who is Pyleah?" I choke out, the blood draining from my face as this is panning out into such a fucking nightmare, I want to hurl.

"She was Queen of the Light Fae. Married to Delinda's uhm…you know…" She shrugs it off as the bile rises in my throat.

"Are you absolutely sure of this?" I bark at her suddenly, regaining my composure as the anger rears up.

She blinks at me and then gives me a scathing look. "Yes. Quite."

We glare at each other for a few moments, when Remiel steps in. "What do you know?" he asks me.

Oh, a whole Hell of a lot. "Nothing. I must go," I blurt and then Astral out, rudely, straight into my father's castle in Shes'Ti, my home Realm.

He glares at me as I intrude. "Rexus. What are you doing here?"

"Is mother still alive?" I snap at him. "Is she still alive, a Light Fae and living in the Light Fae Kingdom with my brother, Blayne?" I count these points off on my fingers.

"Oh, uh…"

I have never seen my father falter in his words before. I

would laugh if this wasn't such a fucking travesty. What the fuck is this all about?

"Yes," he says eventually. "Melisandre is alive and well in the Light Fae Kingdom with your youngest brother."

As he confirms what I already knew, it feels like I have been hit in the gut with a sledgehammer.

"What the actual fuck?" I roar at him, my talons flashing dangerously as I approach him. "How could you keep this from me, from us?"

"Look, I had hoped that you would never find out. How did you anyway?"

"*That* is not what is important right now. Why did you lie to us and say that she, *they*, had died?"

"It's complicated," he says.

I roll my eyes at him. "That really isn't going to deter me." I fold my arms across my chest and wait.

He sighs, flicking his long, blonde hair over his shoulder and then facing off with me. "Fine," he drawls. "Your mother and I were doomed from the start. She is half Light Fae, half Dragon. After the divide, when my Mother decided to fuck everything up, it was forbidden to go anywhere near the Fae, never mind engage in a relationship with one. Sadly, we were in love and even though her father was a Dragon, her mother was a Light Fae, therefore she was never going to be my wife. Her parents were only accepted because they got together before Tiamat tried to overrun the Fae. Although, that didn't last once the Fae Kingdoms were created. Anyway…" He waves his hand as the digression gets back on track, "…Melisandre and I fought over the three of you for days after you hatched. She wanted to take all of you, but that was never going to happen. She needed to go back to the Light Fae. She decided a long time ago to accept that half of her and dismiss her Dragon. She couldn't move here, and I couldn't go there, so we had no choice but to part ways. We eventually agreed that Blayne would go with her and be raised as Light Fae, and that you and Trey'Za would stay here with me and be raised as Dragons."

I swallow, unable to take all of this in. Delinda's Fae mate is my youngest triplet brother.

"Fuck's sake!" I roar at him. "How the fuck? You lied about everything. You said she was a lowly servant that you screwed one night! Now, I find that you were together, that we could have been a real family?"

I clench my fist and punch an ornate vase off the end table, watching it go careening into the wall, next to where Trey is lounging, looking like none of this has come as a shock to him.

"You knew about this?" I shout at him.

He shrugs and pushes off from the wall. "Father, can you leave us to talk?" he asks.

"Yes," Dad says and disappears, taking the easy way out.

Fucker.

The fucking fucker!

"When?" I bark at Trey.

"A few years ago. I wanted to learn more about Mother. I found something of hers in a trunk and cast a spell. It was meant to show me about how she lived while she was here, little snippets of her life. But, seeing as she is still alive, I saw her living her life in the Light Fae Kingdoms with our brother."

"Does she know?"

"No," Trey says with a sigh. "I can't get there and have no way to contact her otherwise."

"And you just accept this? That Dad lied to us and kept our mother and brother away?"

"No, it sucks a pile of shit. I want those Light Fae powers." His eyes gleam with the thought of all that power and I gulp.

The implications of this have just hit me. I, like Delinda, am half Light Fae. Dad must've bound our powers when he decided to raise us as Dragons.

I am about to bend over and puke into a potted plant, when Trey says, "She severed the Chosen connection. How did she do that?"

"How do you know about that?" I ask, wiping my mouth, pushing the nausea aside.

"I felt the bond break. I thought I was dying," he says quietly. "Why would she do that?"

"We agreed that she would to get rid of you and Dad," I say nastily to hurt him.

It works. He flinches and his eyes go sad. "I get it about Dad, although he hasn't mentioned a word of it since he arrived suddenly back home. But me?" He gives me a fierce frown. I can't say anything about that. He can't know that Delinda used her Fae powers on him to make him go away. She told us that in confidence. He can't know she is also half Light Fae. No one can.

"Yes, she didn't want you in her life. She is happy with me," I state.

"And her other two men," he says slyly. "You can't give her everything she is looking for."

"I give her enough."

"Hmm, how are you even still with her if she severed the connection?"

"We created a new bond. One that excludes everyone else." Except Blayne, I growl to myself.

"Interesting," Trey says.

"She loves me," I blurt out, feeling like an idiot. "She wants me to be with her."

"But we could have shared her. Properly this time."

"Oh no!" I snap at him. "We never shared Lianna. You screwed her behind my back!"

He holds his hands up. "How many times do I have to tell you? It was her. I was at your house, waiting for you and she jumped me assuming I *was* you. It's not my fault she couldn't tell us apart, that she didn't know you well enough to know I wasn't you. I was hardly about to push her away. She was a hot piece of ass. I saw no harm in letting her think I was you for a bit of fun. I didn't think you would mind. It's not like we've never done that before."

"She was different," I grit out. "She was my wife."

"But you weren't really in love with her," Trey says.

"Of course, I was! I married her!"

"I mean compared to Delinda. You love her more."

Well, the asshole has me there, but it changes nothing. "You betrayed my trust, and you have done nothing to make up for it since. In fact, last I heard you were still screwing the slut back on Earth. It's why I fucking left!"

He shrugs, infuriating me further. "How did you find out about Mother and Blayne?"

"None of your business," I growl at him.

"So, are we going to ask Dad to unbind our Fae powers now that this is out in the open? I'm betting we can only do it together, so we both have to agree to it."

"What? Are you fucking joking?" He is deluded, seriously.

"No, I am being deadly serious. The only way to get to the Light Fae Kingdom is with those powers."

"I don't want them," I snarl. "It fucking disgusts me…" I pause, remembering that Delinda is also half Light Fae and that I have to be supportive of that. I wonder if she will do the same with me. That's when another thought strikes me. If I do ask for these powers to be unbound, then surely that makes *me* Delinda's Fae mate as well? Yes, and Trey, but he doesn't have the tie-to-life connection with her. I do. I can have it all if I just thought about it for a minute.

I can oust Blayne from her mind and from her life for good. I have the power here, I just need to get over my distaste for the Fae and learn to deal with the fact that I *am* one. Just like my wife. Only that thought makes me start to nod my head and say, "Fine."

38

~PRES~

I'm being a bit creepy and watching my wife as she sleeps. I just can't help it. She is even more beautiful now that she has claimed her throne, if that is possible. I am the luckiest Dragon in all the Realms. Well, one of, anyway.

I cast my glance at To'Kah. He is reading by the fireplace. He likes to read. I find it kind of hot, him being all studious and stuff.

"Stop staring at me," he says, his eyes still on his book and a small smile playing at his lips.

"Stop looking so hot then," I reply with a smirk.

His eyebrows go up and he turns to me. "Oh?" he inquires. "Like what you see, do you?"

"Sure," I say lightly. "I get what Delly sees in you."

He snorts with mirth and goes back to his reading.

I go back to watching my wife sleep.

Today is going to be a difficult day for her. She must step up, in a big way, into a role that, let's be honest, she wasn't ready for. I can feel her anxiety, and I am probably feeding it. I am nervous for her. I have to sort that shit out before she wakes up.

"Go and take a shower," To'Kah says to me, appearing

behind me and putting his hand on my shoulder. "You can't let her know that you are worried. It will make her panic."

"I know," I say with gritted teeth. "I'm trying, but I can't help it."

"Go," he instructs me, hauling me up by my elbow and giving me a shove towards the bathroom.

Half of me thinks he wants to get rid of me so he can be alone with Delinda.

"You need to stop that paranoia, kid," he drawls, annoying me that he has picked up Rex's name for me. "It does no one any good."

"Humph," I mutter and skulk off to the bathroom to duck under the steaming hot jets.

I fume for a few minutes, when I hear the door open.

"Chill out, will you?" To'Kah says to me, knocking on the steamed-up shower door.

"There is only one thing that will make me 'chill out'," I growl at him.

"Delly doesn't want us doing that without her," he replies in a smirky tone. I can't see his face properly, but I know the smirk is there.

"I wasn't talking about you!" I wipe the steam away and glare at him.

He is laughing silently, which goes out loud when he sees me looking at him. "You're an ass," I grumble and go back to my shower.

"Jokes aside, she needs our support, not our worry. She has a big day today," he says, turning serious.

"Yes, I know."

"So, grab your dick and pump away until you find yourself relaxing a bit. Got it?"

I contemplate what he said as I hear him leave and close the door behind him. I look down. I'm rock hard. I seem to have a constant hard-on since I married Delinda. It won't go away. It needs satisfaction every second of every day. I know the other two are slightly more restrained than me,

187

but they have had thousands of years to get some. Me, not so much.

I lather up my hands with the soap and then take my cock in my right hand and close my eyes as I lean on the tiles with my left hand. I can picture Delly doing this to me. Sliding her hand down my shaft and back up again. I imagine her mouth going over the tip and licking slightly, circling me slowly.

I groan and pump harder.

"Fuck," I pant as my balls are already so tight, I am ready to explode.

"Allow me," Delly says.

I open my eyes and see that she has Astralled into the shower with me.

"Jesus," I cry and fall on her, kissing her as I lift her up and shove her against the tiles as I ram my soapy cock into her, hoping it doesn't hurt her or the baby. "I'm sorry," I pant. "I can't wait. I can never wait with you...aaaahhh!" The orgasm hits me like a Dragon in full flight. My cock shoots load after load of cum inside my wife, filling her pussy with my seed until I am drained and ready to go again.

She giggles at me and unwraps her legs from my waist, dropping them down and then pushing me to my knees.

"Taste yourself as you lick my clit," she demands.

"Oh, yes," I groan and part her lower lips so that I have access to that ripe nub that makes her come in pulsing waves when I pinch it with my teeth.

I want that, I want her to come for me, but I am being a selfish prick, as usual. She wants me to see to her first.

I thrust three of my fingers inside her lubricated hole, loving her gasp of desire.

Her hands grip the back of my head, pushing me closer to her sweet, sweet clit. I flick my tongue out and taste the saltiness of my cum. It doesn't put me off; it only makes me want more. I want both of our tastes in my mouth, mingling into a delicious nectar that I could happily live off for the rest of my days.

I slide my free hand up the inside of her thigh, slippery with cum and water from the shower that is beating down on us. I trail it around to her ass and squeeze her cheek hard. She wiggles in rapture, her breathing getting heavier as my tongue works its magick on her clit. She is close, really close. I want my tongue inside her as she comes, so I pull my fingers out and start to rub at her clit as I duck my head further and slide my tongue into her hole.

"Uhh," I groan as she starts to pulse, her cries of lust echoing against the shower tile.

"Fuck, Pres!" she screams, louder and louder as I fuck her with my tongue and keep up the pressure on her clit with my fingers.

I want my dick in her ass so badly, but I refrain as she isn't finished yet. Or rather, she *has* finished and is now on the verge of another climax that rocks through her, causing her knees to buckle.

My hands go up instantly to catch her, but she is already climbing onto my lap and taking my engorged cock in her hand to shove inside her.

She rides me hard, gripping my shoulders tightly, her head thrown back.

"Delly, fuck, Delly," I cry as I unload into her again. "Turn around, please," I beg her.

She giggles again and opens the shower door. We tumble out onto the bathroom mat and she crawls up onto her hands and knees. I part her cheeks and bend over to lick her rear hole, sliding my finger gently into her ass and withdrawing it, stretching the entrance a little bit like Rex taught me how to do.

"I'm so glad you love this," I murmur to her in between licks.

"I'm glad that *you* do," she replies, bringing her fingers up to play with herself as I get myself into position.

"Oh, yes," I breathe. As much as I love pussy sex, ass sex is a hundred times better. I thrust into her, wanting to be a complete savage with her. I want to let loose and not worry about hurting her but stop myself because I know I will if she lets me.

"I love you," I groan, feeling her tight ass sheath my cock, as I bury myself deep inside her. "I love you so much."

"I love you," she whispers back, her breathing going ragged as she brings herself to a climax while I pound into her behind.

"Love me always," I demand of her, needing her to say it, needing desperately to hear it from her lips.

"I will love you always. Always. Always. Always!" Her screams get louder as I crash my hips against her ass, harder and harder.

"Fuck, yes!" I roar as my balls feel like they are about to explode if I don't release into her now. My cum shoots out of me, my cock jerking inside her again and again as I pour everything I have into her. "Delly," I pant. "You are everything."

She pulls away from me and turns to grab my face. She kisses me passionately, her tongue dueling with mine, her breasts pressed up against me, her hips grinding against mine.

"You are my love, my life," she whispers against my lips. "I would die without you."

I choke back the sob that threatens to come out. It is everything I have wanted her to say, but she never has before.

Then she grabs the smashed-up soap off the shower floor and lathers up her hands. She cleans us both up in a tantalizing mix of bubbles and dripping water from the washcloth, before she slides herself back onto my cock and rides me slowly, painfully slowly, circling her hips enticingly as she pushes me back to the floor. She runs her hands up and down my chest, clearly admiring my abs. It makes me smile and openly admire her bouncing tits, her flat stomach, her taut thighs gripping me tightly.

"Gorgeous," I say tweaking her nipples.

She gives me a smug smile, loving the compliment. I don't need her to say it back. I know she thinks the same of me. Her eyes tell me as they hood with desire and then close completely as I make her come in wave after wave of pure pleasure. I could quite happily stay like this with her forever.

39

~DELINDA~

I'm panting with the effort of fucking Pres until he is satisfied. He has the stamina of a thousand men, not to mention the enthusiasm of *ten* thousand men! If he expects this every night, on top of me keeping Rex and To'Kah happy, I will be too exhausted to run this Empire.

Speaking of which…

"I had better get bathed and dressed," I tell my Beta, who is lounging on the bathroom mat with a Cheshire Cat grin on his face.

"Yes, you should. Big day. I will leave you to it. I should thank To'Kah, anyway, for sending you to me."

"I came to you because I felt you needed me, not because To'Kah sent me to you," I chide him, a bit annoyed that he doesn't know this already.

"Oh," he says with a slight blush. "I did need you. Thank you."

"Don't thank me!" I snap at him. "You are my husband. I love you. I want to be with you."

"Sorry," he mumbles, looking abashed.

I am about to yell at him for apologizing, but I give up. I have too much to worry about and do in the next hour. My stomach is in knots, Rex still isn't back from his trip to his father's place, the baby is making me feel even more nauseous than usual and I can sense my mother on the other side of the bedroom door all the way from inside the bathroom. That means one thing. The Fae is out to play and that is never a good sign.

"Go now," I say to him. "And let my mother in, will you?"

He nods and scampers off to do my bidding, letting my mother sweep in on an icy ripple before she slams the bathroom door shut.

"What bit you on the ass?" I ask her as I climb back into the shower that has been steaming up the bathroom for the last half an hour or more.

"Your father," she bites out. "He is an overbearing control freak."

"Well, I can't argue with that, so don't come to me if you're looking for someone to refute you."

"Humph," she says and taps her foot.

"What's the problem?" I ask her with a sigh.

"He is always too overprotective of me when I'm pregnant! It drives me nuts," she grouses.

"Oh," I splutter, glad that I am in the shower and she can't see my red face. I really don't want to know what it is she is complaining about, exactly, but I can guess. "So, back to me…"

"Yes! You!" Through the misty glass, I see her sit herself on the side of the bathtub and fold her arms. "Oh, Delly, I am so proud of you. You have taken your rightful place; you are married with a baby on the way. You are becoming the woman I always knew you could be."

"Thanks," I say with a smug smile. "Bet you didn't picture it *exactly* like this though?"

She snorts. "No, but I know you are happy, and who am I to deny you what your heart desires…"

"Why did you stop?" I press after a long moment.

"I'm just glad that you decided to break the Chosen bond

and, well, *choose* to be with your men and not let fate decide that it's not enough for you."

I stop what I am doing and bite the inside of my lip.

"I've been there before and, at the time, I thought it was great, all part of the grand plan. But it fell apart, and I got burned badly in the process. I never want that for you, for any of my children. You have been responsible and adult about this decision and it makes me very proud and I respect you for it."

The tears prick my eyes and for a brief moment I am elated that she feels that way about me, but it all crashes down around me when I remember the voice in my head. I should tell her, but after what she just said, I can't. I don't want to spoil it. So instead, I clear my throat and say, "Yes, well, they had to go."

"And the Fae mate?" she asks instantly.

"I don't want that," I say shortly. "I love my men. Pursuing that will only hurt them."

I hear her breathe out in relief. "You know that also pertains to your powers?"

"Yes, I know. We have discussed it. I have told them I won't be using the Fae powers until I have bridged the divide between the races."

Silence.

Then, "That's what you intend to do? I would leave well enough alone, Delly."

I turn off the shower and step out. "It's not your decision. It's also not your heritage. It's mine. This is my plan and I will see it through in time."

She nods slowly. "I'm glad that you recognize that it won't be an instantaneous thing. It will take time and effort and battles fought, won and lost."

"I know," I say and then wave my hand. "I was thinking this dress..." I Astral on a black, floor-length gown with a high collar and pointy sleeves.

"No, it's not you," she says, shaking her head.

I frown and then Astral on a purple dress, still brushing the floor, but with a round neckline and regular sleeves.

"Perfect," she says, her face lighting up. "No shoes."

"What? Why?" I complain.

"You want to appear all ethereal and mystical. Barefoot. But paint your toenails the same color as your dress."

In a swirl of magick, I do as she says.

"Hair up in a tight bun," she adds.

I comply.

Then she magicks up the crown and places it carefully on my head. "Perfect. Where is Rexus, by the way?"

"He went to see his father and brother to make sure the Chosen bond was broken. He should have been back by now though." I frown, but that lightens considerably in the next second. "Oh, he's back."

Mother chuckles at me. "Getting the hang of that new bond now, aren't you?"

"Yes, thank the gods. It was a proper nightmare, but it has all come good now."

"I'm glad. Now, let's go."

"Wait," I gulp. "I need a minute."

She gives me an encouraging smile. "You will be great. Be humble and gracious of the honor and basically the exact opposite of your grandmother."

I stifle my laugh. "*That* I can do."

She opens the bathroom door and leads the way back into the bedroom where I stop dead, a big smile forming on my face.

"Surprise," Mother sings out as I take in To'Kah, the High Priestess from my wedding, Rex and Pres, and Papa looking grim.

"Now?" I ask.

"Yes, now," Uncle D says, also coming into the room. "This needs to be official before you face your subjects."

"Well, okay then," I mutter. He makes it sound like a business transaction. "Are you okay with this?" I ask To'Kah.

195

He nods, a big grin on his face. "I will marry you whenever, wherever, you want me."

I grin at him and take his hands.

The High Priestess gets right down to business and rushes us through the vows at super speed.

"Do you…"

"Yes."

"Do you…"

"Yes."

"You may kiss…"

And it's all over.

Jesus. Not exactly a romantic affair, but it *is* official, and I am ecstatic.

"I love you," I murmur to him as he bends to give me a chaste kiss.

"I love you. Now go and be the Empress for a while."

I chuckle at him and pull away. I head towards the door, expecting everyone else to follow me, when Mother calls out, "*Astral* down."

I'm not happy about that. I wanted the time to gather myself, but I shove the sudden nervousness aside and Astral my ass straight onto the big stage in the Great Hall, and then gulp as I see what's in front of me.

If I thought the place was packed out yesterday, then I was mistaken. All of the chairs have been removed, so it is standing room only and there are twice, thrice, as many Dragons stuffed into here. The noise is deafening, and the sea of faces increases the nausea I have been pushing aside.

My breathing goes shallow. I start to panic and look back, ready to escape, but when I see my family, my husbands, behind me, I stop and relax. I can do this. I *have* to do this.

I face the crowd again and clear my throat, expecting the cacophony to die down.

It doesn't.

It does nothing to help my nerves.

I look back helplessly at my mother and she steps forward and places her hand on my back. "You need to Shift."

I look at her askance "I can't. The baby…"

"You have Shifted recently, and the baby has been fine. I know it seems weird with you changing shape, but all will be well, I assure you."

I nod and trust her. She wouldn't steer me wrong about this, and she is right. I *have* Shifted a few times before I found out I was pregnant, and I know the baby is still safe and sound.

I take the crown off my head and hand it to To'Kah.

Then I whip my dress over my head and shove it at Rex, who growls his disapproval at me. I turn to face the horde of Dragons completely naked. I thought, if anything, that would make me want to run and hide, but nope. It does the exact opposite. I *want* to be standing here naked and in all my glory. I want them to see me as I am. I want them to admire me. I want to be lusted after but knowing that I am off limits. It makes me feel a power that has nothing to do with my magickal powers. It's all about woman-power.

I am smokin' hot.

I have a killer body; a rack that my husbands can't keep their hands, and mouths, off. I *should* be showing off to anyone who will look.

I have a Power that none of the subjects before me will ever have.

I have never felt so invincible in my entire life.

I fucking love it!

Oh yes, Princess. You are glorious. Take what is yours, for soon it will be ours.

I give them all a wicked smile, having caught the attention of the majority of the room.

I know my husbands are not pleased that I am standing here with my bits on show to every single Dragon in the Fortress, but tough. I am not even bothered that my parents and Uncle are standing behind me, although I am sure they are looking anywhere but at my pert, bare ass.

Then I drop to my knees and a reverent hush goes over the room, quietening the rest that hadn't yet noticed me.

I start the Shift slowly. I want them all to see, to *experience* it with me. I let my wings sprout, uncurling leisurely until they are glowing golden in the Great Hall. My talons scrape across the ancient stone floor as they spring free. The golden scales ripple down my sides as I let myself change shape. My neck elongating, my skull changing shape. I flash my fangs at the crowd and then I am standing thirty feet tall, the only Golden Dragon to exist, with a few thousand pairs of eyes on me.

I swish my tail, careful not to knock my family off the platform, and curl it around me. I duck my head and puff out a stream of smoke that gets in the faces of the few hundred Dragons at the front, and then I lift my head up quickly and let out an eardrum-bursting shriek and a stream of fire at the high ceiling.

I look back down, and see that everyone is gawking up at me, but then lower their eyes and bow their heads when they see me notice them.

Now this is more like it!

Time to Shift back.

I do so quickly and give my husbands a break by Astralling my dress back on quickly, allowing To'Kah to replace my crown.

"Now that I have your attention," I say loudly and clearly. "Let me say that I am honored to be standing in front of you today as your Empress. I do not take this responsibility and great privilege lightly. I will do everything in my Power to make you proud that I am your Empress, however there will be some changes in the coming weeks. I hope that we can work together to make the running of the Realms an effortless task, and I hope that I can count on every one of you to be proud, upstanding and loyal subjects. I will do my very best to reign over you fairly, with dignity, respect and mercy."

"Here, here," Rex shouts out behind me.

I give a half smile.

"Long live the Empress," Pres calls out.

"Long may She reign," To'Kah adds loudly.

The words are repeated over and over for a few minutes before Uncle D steps in.

"We will now have the Grievances Assembly. Those of you who do not wish an audience with the Empress, are free to attend the Reception in the Dining Hall."

I give him a surprised look. "Wait? What?" I ask. "Grievances Assembly?"

My shoulders sag slightly before Mother pokes me in the back and I straighten up.

"That's right," Uncle D says with a smug smile which does nothing to quell the sudden knowledge that he did this on purpose.

"You ass," I grumble at him, making him laugh.

"Have fun!" he calls and Astrals off, leaving me to face off with way more, now irate, Dragons than I had hoped there would be.

I turn to look at my husbands, expecting them to have my back, but with small, apologetic smiles, they Astral off, along with my parents, leaving me, the Empress, to deal with my subjects' problems.

Great, guys.

Thanks a fucking bunch.

A very long time later, I am still mediating a territory dispute in a Realm I have never even been to. It reminds me that I must make some trips out and very soon. I also want to meet Pres's father. I'm not in the least bit happy that I've already had the honor of meeting Rexus's. I already know To'Kah's father so that isn't an issue that needs addressing. However, there *is* a pressing issue that needs dealing with, and soon, with regard to my newest husband. I still haven't confronted him about the decision he made for Uncle D to kill him in order to light a fire under my ass. Before we can even think about consummating this union, I will have to yell at him about it. For a very long time.

"Your Highness?"

"Hm?" I draw my attention back to the two male Dragons that have been duking it out over this piece of land for the last two hours. "I rule in your favor," I tell the Dragon peering at me with bright green eyes from under a thatch of yellow hair. "It was your land first."

"But, Your Highness," the other one protests. "My orchard has been there for years. They can't just take it back."

"Yes, they can. They may have had no need for the land in the past and were kind enough to let you have it. Now, they need to extend their home. You will just have to move your orchard somewhere else."

He gapes at me.

"Your Empress has spoken," Uncle D booms out from behind me. "Dismissed."

They scamper off and I sigh.

Uncle D turns to me, slumped in my throne, my crown all askew, and laughs and laughs and laughs so hard, I think his sides are going to split. "Oh, Delinda," he snorts in between guffaws. "You are too precious."

"What?" I ask in a huff, pissed off with his raucous laughter at my expense.

"Such a rookie mistake," he splutters.

"You are the one who made me do this!" I expostulate, stamping my foot.

"I didn't expect you to sit here for hours on end listening to all of them. You have missed half of your own Reception!"

"Then what was I supposed to do?" I cry in frustration.

"Be an Empress," he states, going serious. "I have been

putting those two off for about five years! You either delegate or tell them to come back later."

"I can't do that!" I exclaim. "I just told them I would be a fair ruler."

"Girl, they don't expect you to sit here and judge every case on your own. You have surprised and pleased your subjects far beyond anything I have seen in a while. You have made a wonderful impression on them, but you will be bogged down for eternity with trivialities if you insist on doing this all on your own."

"I don't want to do it on my own. I have plans to hire delegates," I protest.

"Good. But this was a lesson that I needed to teach you. While you have impressed the Empire by taking your duty seriously, you have failed yourself by allowing them to take advantage of you."

"Oh," I say so deflated, I feel like crawling under the duvet and never coming back out.

He strokes my hair and says kindly, "Next time. Now go and be with your family. They are waiting for you."

I slope off, really not wanting to be in anyone's company right now. I wanted to excel out of the gate with this Empress thing. Seems I have so much more to learn than I thought.

I find To'Kah first. In fact, he is waiting for me at the entrance to the Dining Hall.

"Wife," he says to me, bending down to kiss me.

I scowl at him and turn my head, so his lips land on my cheek.

He freezes and then says, "Ah. We need to talk."

"Damn straight we do. How could you? You made an awful, selfish decision that affected me *and* our child. It was unfair and...and dreadful of you."

"I know," he says, and takes me by my elbow, leading me away into a small alcove off the huge foyer. "I made it in the spur of the moment to help you, but I realize now what a terrible decision it was. Had I known about the baby before, I would never have agreed to it."

"That changes nothing," I snarl at him. "You chose to leave me. Just when things were finally good with us, just when we could finally be together out in the open, you decided to leave me. It makes me think that you don't really want me, that you are only here now because of the baby." I have tears in my eyes, and I start to snivel.

"Oh, Delly," he says desperately, squeezing my hands hard. "You know that isn't true. All I have ever wanted is to be with you. I adore you. I worship you and I couldn't imagine my life without you in it. Without *Her* in it. I'm so sorry for my rash decision. I will never leave you again, I promise you."

He kisses my tears away, and I let him.

He has alleviated the fears that suddenly rose up out of nowhere.

"I need you," I whisper to him. "My Dragon needs you."

His face lights up, his eyes swimming with happiness and love. I know that he separates us in his mind. I know that he loves Her and that I am just part of that package. It's okay. I don't mind it, much. I have Rex and Pres to love *me*. To them, *I* am everything and She is part of my package.

"Why do you think that?" To'Kah asks me seriously.

Aw shit. I forgot about the bond and I had no mental blocks up.

I shrug, uncomfortable that he has read my thoughts on this.

"It isn't true, Delinda. I love you. Yes, as far as I am concerned you are separate from Her, and I do love Her, very much. I am bonded with Her just as much as I am with you, maybe more so because of what we share, that is just ours. I can't explain it to you, but when She is inside me, I feel whole. It doesn't mean that I don't love you. I love you more than anything and I would even without Her. You are my everything, but She is everything to my Dragon. Do you understand what I'm trying to say?" He looks petrified that I am going to say 'no'. I do get it, now that he has explained it to me. I wish he had done that earlier. I have rarely seen a vulnerable side to him, and it makes me love him even more.

"Yes. Now, She needs balancing. It has been a rollercoaster this last week, and we have neglected Her."

He nods eagerly and Astrals us off to the bedroom.

"Wait," I say, putting my hand up. "I want Rex and Pres to see it. To be a part of it. I don't want them left out of such an important act between us."

"I'll go and get them," he says and disappears, returning quickly with my other two husbands.

"We have talked about this, and we are prepared to let you two be alone together, just this once," Rex says, before anyone can blink.

"This isn't about that," I say, "But thank you. I don't think we will take you up on it, though."

To'Kah shakes his head in agreement, to their obvious relief.

"What is it then?" Pres asks.

"To'Kah is going to balance my Power. I want you to always be with us for it. I don't want you to ever think that it is something that we share that is outside of our collective relationship."

They both nod, as eager to see it as To'Kah is to perform it.

"And then, when we make love afterwards, I want all of us joined together," I say, watching for their reaction.

I see their excitement and it makes me shiver inside. They are desperate for it after I have withheld permission the last couple of times. I feel a pang of nerves from Pres, and so do the other two men, but Rex gives him a gentle elbow in the side and a soft smile. "We'll go easy on you," he says kindly.

Pres nods and licks his lips, his eyes on me. "Tell me what you want from me," he says.

I give him a slow, sexy smile as the permission has been

given to corrupt the living daylights out of my little Beta. Rex chuckles as To'Kah hides his smile.

I turn away from them then and strip off. The Noble One needs Her Guardian. Now.

To'Kah is behind me in an instant, naked and aroused beyond belief. He runs his hands down my back and She ripples with delight. It makes my nipples pucker and my back teeth tingle.

"You are so beautiful," he murmurs to Her. "I have missed you. Come to me, my love."

My breath catches in my throat. It is the first time he has ever said these words out loud. He has probably said them a million times in his head. He starts to draw Her into himself, peeling Her off my back. She is sending out a brilliant golden glow as Her wings flap gently.

Once She is gone, I turn around and watch as To'Kah balances the Power of the Dragon Empress for the very first time. His head is thrown back, his long, dark hair flying in the breeze. His eyes are closed and the look of utter contentment and bliss on his face is a sight to behold.

Rex and Pres seem taken aback slightly by the sheer intimacy of the act. They have seen it before when the Dragon was going wild, but this is something entirely different. It is slow, languorous even. He is connecting with Her on a level that thrills me to my very core.

"I love you too," he murmurs, shocking me.

She speaks to him? How? Since when? He kept that fucking quiet. She doesn't even speak to *me* and She is mine.

His erection is so fierce, it is bouncing with the need to detonate in a Realm-shattering climax. I want to suck him off while he still has my Dragon inside of him. It is wicked, but I know he will love it.

I sink to my knees and take his cock in my hand. His breath rasps and then lets out a guttural moan as I take him in my mouth.

"Delly," he croaks out. "I can't hold...fuuuuuuck!"

He shoots his load, his cock jerking forcefully as he pumps his cum into my mouth. I swallow, but he isn't finished yet. It's almost like his orgasm doubled up and he is coming again.

"Sweet Jesus!" he cries, as my mouth works overtime to take his full size in as he drains himself down the back of my throat. "I love you. I love you. I love you," he pants, thrusting his hips, fucking my mouth. "Rise now," he commands me.

I do as he says because I know he needs to let go of the Dragon immediately. She has too much Power for him to hold for very long. What I did was dangerous for him, but there is no denying that he wanted it, regardless of the risk to him.

He replaces Her quickly and before She has even settled, he grabs me and spins me around to kiss me fervently, before Rex and Pres join us.

I drop to the rug with To'Kah still kissing me, his hands kneading my breasts. "That was…thank you," he whispers against my lips. "I can't even tell you how much that meant."

"I know how much. That's why I did it," I reply with a loving smile, brushing his hair off his face and then bunching my fist into it so that I can bring his lips back to mine.

I kiss him, enjoying the sweetness of it, while Rex finger fucks me slowly. I am slippery with my juices already, needing some hotter action. I pull away from To'Kah and push his head towards Rex.

"Kiss," I demand and then sit back to watch them lock lips. They are both excellent kissers, so I can only imagine what that must feel like for them. I can see their tongues darting in and out; it's making my mouth water. Pres has taken over finger fucking me, occasionally ducking his head to lick me as well.

"Oh, yes," I moan.

Rex is trailing his hands over To'Kah's hard body, lower and lower until he reaches the enormous erection standing in between them proudly.

To'Kah catches his breath as Rex grabs him and tugs, jerking him off slowly, circling his palm over the tip before he goes back to sliding his hand up and down.

"Now, I want you to suck him off," I murmur.

Rex smirks and ducks his head.

"No, not you," I whisper, sitting up and pushing Pres back to the floor. I straddle him and he wastes no time in sliding his dick into me. I ride him slowly, my eyes on my other two husbands. Rex is now lying down and To'Kah is bending over him, his lips millimeters from taking my Alpha in his mouth.

"Fuck," Rex groans as To'Kah's lips encase his huge cock. He is twitching, eager to climax, but I know he will hold off for as long as he possibly can. He has wanted To'Kah's mouth around his dick for a long time; he will want to savor this, as he should.

"More," I gasp, speeding up my own actions, ready to come around Pres in a pulsing, wet heat that makes me arch my back as it rushes through me.

"Do not come yet," I warn Pres. "I have plans for us."

His blue eyes go darker as he thinks of the possibilities.

"Stand up now," I instruct them.

They pull away, Rex looking reluctant to do as I ask, but does it anyway.

"And you," I say to Pres, climbing off him.

I kneel on the floor and wave my hand in a circle. They get my meaning and surround me, cocks in hand.

They start to jerk themselves off as I watch them hungrily, waiting for them to come all over me in a shower of salty goodness.

"All together," I murmur, knowing that the instruction will be difficult for them to co-ordinate. But it's what I want. "Tell me when you are close."

"Close," Pres cries, his hand furiously working his shaft up and down.

"Mm, same," Rex murmurs, his eyes on me, enjoying this as much as I am.

"I'm ready," To'Kah pants, his hand going still has he groans out loud, spurting his come all over my face as I turn to him. I close my eyes and feel the warm splats landing on my cheeks and lips.

I turn as the stream of cum that Pres fires at me, lands on my face and tits, mingling with Rex's as he is the last to let go completely.

"Fuck, you are gorgeous," Rex says to me, kneeling down and licking the cum off my face before plunging his tongue into my mouth so that I can taste all of us.

To'Kah is sliding his hands over my nipples, slippery with the product of their orgasms.

Pres has found my nether regions again, his lubed-up fingers, thrusting into my ass as I bend over, taking my other lovers with me as I move.

"What are you ready for?" I ask over my shoulder at my Beta.

He goes bright red. "I will fuck, but I'm not ready to be fucked yet. At least not in the ass."

"That's fine," Rex says, reassuring him. "Only do what you feel comfortable with. But, right now, I think our lady wants to make this an anal train, am I right?"

I nod with glee, glad that he read my mind.

"So, that makes Delinda at the front, with you at the back and me and Rex in the middle," To'Kah states as if this is the most natural thing in the World. "So, it's up to you to decide who you want to fuck," he says to Pres. "And, Delly, who you want to fuck you."

"I don't care," I say quickly. "Pres?"

He licks his lips. "Surprise me," he says after a beat.

Rex chuckles. "Well, as much as I want to pound you

again," he says to To'Kah, "I want to feel your cock in my ass as I fuck our wife in hers. So, how about it, Pres? To'Kah?"

They both nod and then no more words are spoken as we arrange ourselves to show how we need each other. I bend over, resting my hands on the edge of the bed and wait for Rex to lube me up some more. He presses his tip at my rear hole and gently eases himself inside me, making me gasp. He is huge, so turned on by this. I feel him brace himself with his foot on the bed. As inspiration hits me, I cast a mirror spell so that I can see what is happening behind me. I think we may have to invest in some massive mirrors on the ceiling above the bed, on the wall, all around.

I watch Rex's face as To'Kah, dick in hand, pushes himself into Rex's ass.

"Oh, yes," Rex says, going completely still.

This is going to take some co-ordination on our behalf so we must wait until Pres has impaled To'Kah onto his cock.

"Do it," To'Kah says to him softly. "I want to feel you fucking me."

"Shit," Pres says desperately. "Fuck."

A few seconds later, we are all riding the anal train to sheer ecstasy.

"Jesus," I pant, being shoved forward by the weight of the men behind me. Rex is thrusting into me as To'Kah rides his ass, with Pres hammering into him.

"Fuck," Pres breathes. "I'm coming…"

I move my fingers up to my clit to bring myself to a sexy-as-fuck orgasm that makes me tremble and sweat at the same moment that Rex shoots his load into me.

"Uhh," To'Kah groans, climaxing into Rex and then we all collapse in a heap on the floor, grinning at each other as we catch our breath.

"How was that for you?" I ask Pres, taking his hand and lacing our fingers together.

"Good," he says with a nervous laugh. "Great. Fucking amazing."

Rex snorts. "Yeah, get it right, kid. Next time we do that, I want you ready for me to fuck you."

Pres bites his lip but nods stoically.

I giggle at him as Rex is only teasing him.

To'Kah gets up and disappears, returning shortly with a washcloth. He goes about cleaning me up. I am sticky with semen and sweat, as are they. He turns to the men and goes about cleaning them up as well with a separate washcloth.

"Wow, you are handy, aren't you?" I say with a laugh.

"Just being considerate. We are nowhere near finished with each other yet," he says in a sinfully delicious tone that makes me damp and crawl over to him.

I tangle my fingers into his black, silky hair and whisper. "No, we are not, *husband*.

40

~TO'KAH~

I gaze into her eyes. My wife. I still can't believe that this has happened. It seems almost surreal, like a dream that I don't want to wake up from.

I bend down to kiss her, scooping her up in my arms and lifting her up. She is so tiny next to me, it makes me want to cherish her, even though she can kick my ass into the middle of the next Realm.

"I love you, my wife," I murmur to her. "I need you now."

"I know," she replies, and she does know.

She knows that while I am more than okay with what is evolving in my relationship with the men. I want it, desire it, crave it even, I need to assert myself on her afterwards. If she is worried that I will go off and be with one of them on our own, she needn't. I won't ever do that. Not only because of how she sees it, but because of how *I* see it. Doing this with her involvement sits well with me. I couldn't imagine being with one of the men without her. What we have shared today, has been a very intimate connection between us all. But now I need that intimacy just from her.

"Let me love you," she whispers.

I nod and lie back on the rug, reveling in the attention of her hands and mouth.

The men leave us alone for now. We need to consummate our marriage and they know that it has to be just for us. I don't care if they watch us, in fact, I want them to watch us. I just want my new wife to myself for this one time.

Her mouth closes over my cock and I sigh with happiness. Her lips and tongue slide over my length, her hand cupping my balls and squeezing tightly before she releases me, teasing me to the point where I don't think I can hold on anymore.

I pant with the effort. I don't wish to come in her mouth. I want to flood her pussy as she rides me with that sweet abandon that is just hers. I want to watch her tits bouncing, I want to feel her clit on my fingertips. I need to feel her clench around me. She has taken complete control of me, of my body, my heart and I let her. I had every intention of impaling her and fucking her until I couldn't breathe anymore. But this is so much better.

I groan as she hisses at me.

"Come now," she demands.

"Sorry, Delly, not going to happen yet," I reply with a smile.

"Grrr," she growls at me. "Going to make me work for it?"

"No, I just know where I want you when I do pump out so much cum it will fill you up completely."

"Aah," she cries softly.

I smirk at her. I knew it would turn her on in ways that I need from her. She crawls up me, positioning that sweet pussy of hers over my dick. She grabs me and slides down excruciatingly slowly.

"Now," she commands.

"No."

"Now!" She digs her nails into my abs so hard, I feel that she is going to let loose those wicked talons of hers.

"Not yet. Ride me, Princess."

"Why are you dictating to me?" she asks, slowing to a halt and putting her hands on her hips.

I search her eyes at her words, but I can see that she is playing with me.

So, I play back. "Not many men can say that they have the Empress serve them so well."

"Oooh," she practically hisses at me, her eyes narrowed. "You like having that power?"

"You have no idea," I retort, hearing the men stifle their snorts of amusement. "I want that pretty cunt of yours to do all of the work, *Your Highness*."

She gasps at my coarse language, but her arousal has gone off the charts. I can smell it. I can feel it. She is sopping wet as she starts to move again. Slowly, to show me that she is in charge despite my attitude towards this. Then she does exactly what I knew she would, and it makes me laugh.

She climbs off me, leaving my raging cock dripping with her juices and twitching furiously to be back inside her. "This pretty cunt isn't here to serve you," she states.

"Oh, yes, it is," I inform her. "You are now my wife. That takes precedence over you being Empress."

Rex lets out a loud guffaw as Pres just stares at me in horror.

She smirks at me. "Well, never let it be said that I wasn't a dutiful *wife*," she drawls. She crouches over me, her pussy millimeters from the tip of my aching cock.

Then she slowly lowers herself down, but not taking me inside her. She flattens my cock against me, pressing her wet heat onto it and then sliding up and down as she teases me mercilessly.

"Oh, fuck, Delly," I cry out, savoring the feel of her.

She reaches down to play with her clit as she pleasures herself on me, using me.

"Do you want more?"

"Yes," I pant. "I want more."

She leans over and wiggles her hips, pressing her lips to mine.

"More," I rasp.

She circles her hips.

I am desperate to grab her and force her onto my cock, but I restrain myself. This is all for her.

She smiles down into my eyes. "I'm ready for you," she says and lifts her hips slightly.

"Thank fuck for that," I groan, grabbing my dick and guiding it into her.

She has taken this game and turned it on its head. She doesn't move a muscle, making me jerk up to thrust into her. I grab her hips for leverage and pound into her, my eyes on hers until she can't resist slamming herself down, engulfing my length up to my balls.

"Fuck," I breathe as she lifts up and does it again.

And again.

She comes suddenly, crying out, and this is what I needed. I needed to feel her hot, dripping pussy clenching around me after our exploits earlier.

I sit up, wrapping my arms around her and roll us over so that she is underneath me.

I brace myself on my hands and pound into her, forgetting about restraint. She can handle it. She would tell me if she couldn't. I nail her so hard; she screams and writhes under me.

It is too much for the men to bear. They have joined us now, kneeling over her, jerking off over her face as I hammer into her with all the force of the ancient Dragon that I am. It is the thought of the savage Dragon mating that we will engage in soon that pushes me over the edge. I yell out in victory as my dick fires its juice into her, causing Rex and Pres to come all over her face, a fair deal of it going all over me in the process.

"I love this," she cries, taking her hands and smearing the cum down her face, her neck and over her breasts. "Use me. All of you. Use me. Cover me in your desire before you use me so hard, I am nothing but a rag doll in your arms. Give me no mercy. Keep going until there is nothing left."

"Oh, fuck," we all moan in response to her words, and proceed to give her exactly what she asked for.

41

~DELINDA~

The days have rolled into weeks. I have settled into my role and hired delegates to do the grunt work. It was right in front of me the entire time, but took Rex to fill me in.

I have used my husbands to hand off the day-to-day stuff to.

Rex is in charge of the business side of this Empire. I found out, when he was quick to *point* out, that he has attended several prestigious universities on Earth over the centuries and has a dozen degrees in everything to do with business, economics and commerce.

Pres oversees the magickal side of things. He is my head sorcerer. His confidence when he conducts his magick is beyond arousing. But as soon as we get back into the bedroom, he turns into the shy, cute little puppy that I fell in love with. That is also arousing as fuck. I love making him do things that he has never done before. I love pushing him out of his comfort zone. Although, at this point, there is precious little left that we can corrupt him with. Only that one thing that he isn't ready for yet, but that's fine. Rex will treat him gently when the time is right. My Alpha is dying to get his dick into my Beta's ass, and it will happen soon, I have no doubt.

So, that leaves To'Kah, and, of course, he is in charge of the Guardians, Guardians-in-training and all things of that nature.

On this day, I am sitting at my desk in my office, staring at a stack of files that I wish I could hand off, but I said I would deal with the grievances and to my credit, I have. However, it all gets put into writing so that I can attend to it at my own convenience. It is a system that bucks tradition, but my subjects seem to have gotten over the horror of putting pen to paper to air their issues and plied me with enough problems to last me years, it seems.

I put my hand to my mouth and stifle the urge to retch into the desk drawer. My morning sickness, well, all-of-the-time sickness, hasn't abated even though I am verging on four months along. The time is ripe for To'Kah and I to announce the pregnancy. I am starting to show. Only slightly; you wouldn't notice if you didn't know my body the way I, or my men, do. It makes me proud. I can't wait to sport a big bump that tells the Empire that I have created life with the love of my life. Well, *one* of the loves of my life. The downside, apart from the nausea, is the fact that any rough sex has gone out of the window now that it is becoming more obvious that I am growing a baby inside me. My husbands refuse to treat me in the way that I wish they would sometimes. I love to dominate them, be in control as I bring them to their knees, but sometimes a girl just wants to be treated like a whore.

I sigh and try to focus on the dispute in front of me.

A knock at the door brings a welcome respite.

I am quick to call out, "Enter!"

I peer at the doorway when an eye-wateringly gorgeous woman approaches me.

"Your Highness," she says, curtsying deep and low.

"And you are?" I ask her, taking in her hotness with a critical eye. She is something else altogether to look at. Long, blonde tresses, bright green eyes, a rack that is more than just a handful.

"Here to serve, Ma'am," she replies with lowered eyes. "I have traveled from Shes'Ti to offer you my oath and to swear my loyalty to your reign."

"Okay," I say. Something seems a bit off about this. No one else has bothered with such formalities. "Are you wishing to stay in Vaskah?"

"Yes, Your Highness. Any service that you have for me will be met with enthusiasm and appreciation."

"Fine, go and find my husband, Rexus. He will find you a place to stay. Your name?"

Her eyes meet mine for the very first time. "Lianna, Your Highness," she states and then backs out, closing the door behind her.

"Hmm," I mutter, still pondering this woman that has shown up on my doorstep.

A few minutes later there is another knock at the door. I frown at it this time, annoyed. What is this? Disturb the Empress day or something? "Yes?" I call out anyway.

It opens and Rex walks in. I frown at him, because why is he knocking, but then I look harder and grimace. "What do *you* want?" I ask Trey. "Weren't you banished or something?"

He chuckles. "Not quite," he says. "I'm back and I wanted you to be the first to know."

"Gee, I'm honored," I drawl. "So, Rex doesn't know you are here yet?"

"No," he says, giving me a sad look. "I was upset that you broke the Chosen bond, Your Highness. That wasn't fair."

"It wasn't fair of you to deceive me into thinking you were Rex," I reply.

He shrugs. "A ruse I am familiar with, as is he. How *can* you tell us apart, by the way? Not many can save for our father."

"Ugh, don't remind me of him," I spit out. "I didn't at first, but now that I know he has a twin, I can see the subtle

217

differences. He is more arrogant..." He lets out a loud guffaw, "...yet his eyes are more open. With me anyway. You are quite closed off. But the main thing is, he has endearments for me. You don't."

"Hm," he mutters. "Noted."

I narrow my eyes at him. "Don't think you can pull that shit twice."

"Oh, I wouldn't dream of it," he says, sitting down and propping his feet up on my desk, to my annoyance. "You know, his first wife couldn't tell us apart."

That grenade lands right where I think he meant it to, judging by the smug look on his face. He suspects, correctly, I might add, that Rex hasn't told me about that. My heart feels like it is about to explode with jealousy and anger that he kept it from me.

"So, I've heard," I drawl, hoping that he can't tell that I am lying.

"Hehe," he chuckles. "He has such a type, it's hilarious."

"Oh? And what's that then? Dragon Empresses are few and far between."

"Sassy," he smirks. "I like you a lot, Delinda. No, I mean gorgeous, green-eyed blondes with racks to die for."

I gulp. That not only describes me, but the hot blonde who was in here before Trey showed up. I am going to have to keep an eye on that bitch. I mentally kick my ass because I just sent her straight to my husband. What a fuckwit.

"And yours?" I ask to deflect.

"Same," he replies blandly. "We are twins in every way."

"I doubt you could live up to his standards," I comment, quite enjoying this banter even though I should be shoving him into the pit for trying to do exactly that to his own twin. "He is quite the monster in the sack," I add.

"So am I. You would know if you gave me half a chance. I thought women liked the fantasy of twins. You could make it a reality, you know."

"Never," I say mildly. "Rex doesn't want you in my life, so

you won't be. As far as the fantasy goes, sure, I guess it's kinda hot, but I prefer triplets."

His eyes flash with raw lust at that comment that was meant to insult, not arouse. Asshole. At least I know he can't pull a third look-a-like out of the bag, so he's fucked as far as I am concerned

"Oh, really," he says slowly. "Well, I'll be damned."

"Leave now," I dismiss him casually. "I have Empress stuff to do."

"Think about what I said," he says quietly, standing up and leaning over my desk, his brown eyes boring into mine. "Imagine what it would be like to have two of us attending to your every need."

"I already have three men attending to my every need, as well as their own. You up for that, Trey?" I lay down the challenge and hope that I have him pegged correctly that he is *nothing* like my husband.

He licks his lips and narrows his eyes at me, clearly not enjoying the mental picture as I expected.

"Yeah, didn't think so," I scoff. "Go now and don't hassle me again."

"I'm game for anything," he says after a beat. "Could be kinda interesting."

"Not. Interested," I grit out.

"We'll see," he says, grabbing my hand and kissing it before I can pull it away. "You have no idea what I can bring to the table."

"Humph," I mutter rudely and watch him vanish from my office.

I sit back and contemplate what he said about Rex's first wife. Why didn't he tell me? Is it because he still loves her, or because it was so inconsequential that it meant nothing to him? Either way, it is obvious that Trey had a crack at her, and Rex didn't like it. I wonder if that's why they aren't together anymore. Or maybe they were, and I got in the way? I swallow loudly at that thought. Only one way to sort this out. I am going to have to confront my Alpha about his secrets.

J don't have any trouble finding Rex. He is about fifty meters from my office, hissing at that Lianna woman, and I do mean literally *hissing* at her. His Dragon tongue and talons have come out to play. I never knew you could get a partial Shift with your other tongue. Oh, the possibilities are endless…

Wait. I shake my head. *Get a grip, woman.*

He senses me way before he sees me, that much is clear, as he straightens up and puts the Dragon bits away. He turns to me, giving me that glorious smile that makes me more suspicious than wet in the panty region.

"Princess," he says smoothly. "Everything okay?"

"Did you know Trey was here?" I bark at him, giving the Lianna bitch a scathing look that lets her know exactly what I think of her standing here with my Alpha husband.

"Err, I just found out," he says, also giving Lianna a scathing look. "He came to you?" He frowns at me.

"Yes, he is being quite overt about his intentions now. Deal with him, before I do."

"Yes, Ma'am," he smirks at me.

"And *you*," I aim at Lianna. "What is it you want with my husband?"

Rex looks between the two of us and grabs my elbow. "You sent her to me to find her a place to stay," he reminds me. "Although, I think we should refrain from taking on new members to the Fortress without doing a thorough check on them."

Lianna gives him such a filthy look, I can't help but think there is more to this. She is awfully bold in her hatred considering she has just met the man. Or has she…?

"Do you two know each other?" I inquire, pseudo-sweetly.

"No," Rex says hastily. "About Trey, we should discuss that in private."

"Agreed," I say and turn back to Lianna. "Dismissed."

"But…"

"I wasn't suggesting before that you stay *here*," I inform her. "Rex, sort her out a place to stay elsewhere. Then, you come and find me. We have things to discuss."

"Of course," he murmurs and drops his head to kiss my lips chastely.

Then, he roughly takes hold of Lianna's elbow and steers her quickly away from me.

"Trouble in paradise?" Trey asks, sidling up to me, glaring after Rex and Lianna.

I plaster a smile on my face. "No. Unless you count you showing up here. Rex isn't pleased."

"Really? I thought we reached an understanding when he came to see me a few weeks ago." He boxes me in, invading my personal space so that I have to step back and hit the wall behind me. I give him a hard shove on his chest, glad that the Chosen bond is well and truly severed.

"Go home," I snarl at him.

"Nope, not leaving until you give in. One night is all I need to convince you."

"In your dreams, asshole, now I suggest you fuck off before Rex finds you with me."

I Astral off, regardless of my words to him and impatiently wait for Rex to come to me and start explaining himself.

42

~REX~

"You need to leave, right now," I hiss at my ex-wife. "How dare you show up here and interact with the Empress behind my back."

I shove her forward and she turns to face me with that look on her face that used to make me beg to be with her. Now, I am so turned off by her, I want her gone. Delinda is no fool, she knows something is up and I'll have to come clean. But I really don't want to. I wanted this part of my past dead and buried.

"I wanted to meet the woman who took my place," she snarls. "I'm impressed, Rex, you sure went straight to the top, didn't you?"

"I love her," I state, but have no idea why I need to defend myself to this harlot.

"Sure, and everything she can give you, all that power you crave is just a plus, right?"

"You have no idea what you are talking about. You don't know me anymore, Li, and you sure as fuck don't *get* to know me anymore. You made sure of that when you fucked Trey behind my back."

Her green eyes go furious. "How many times do I have to tell you, I didn't know it was him?"

"That's even worse, Li, don't you get it? You couldn't even tell us apart? I'd rather you said you knew it was him. Maybe *that* I could've gotten past."

"Can *she* tell you apart?" she asks snidely. "Trey wants her, don't make the mistake of thinking he won't try it."

"He already did, and Delinda knew it wasn't me. See, Li, she *knows* me. She *loves* me. Trey won't come between us because he has no power here."

"Don't be so sure. He brought me here for a reason," she says.

I sigh. I shouldn't be surprised by that. Of course it was Trey that made this grave error in judgment. As soon as Delinda finds out who Lianna is, she is going to hit the fucking roof. Luckily, Trey will be in the firing line and hopefully I will get away with just not telling her I had a wife before her.

I shake my head to myself. Who the fuck am I kidding?

I am dead.

Deader than dead.

She is going to throw me in the fire pit, and nothing is going to save my ass from burning.

"Whatever that reason is, she won't fall for it," I state, trying to convince myself of this. If I get to her now, I can hopefully salvage the wreckage of her trust before it vanishes completely. "Now leave and don't come back."

I stalk off, needing to get to Delinda. I probably should've stayed to make sure Lianna fucked off, but I don't have the time. I have already kept Delinda waiting for far too long.

I Astral out, mid-stride, and land next to her, making her jump, and clench her fists in my face with a grimace so fierce it must be giving her a headache.

I grab her fists before she can beat me to death with them. "Let me explain," I start.

"No, really, it's a bit late for that. You were married before?" she asks, her face a hurt mask that rips at my heart. "Why didn't you tell me?"

"I was going to, but our marriage was so quick, I didn't really have the time and then afterwards it seemed pointless. It was over a very long time ago, long before you were even born."

"You think that makes it okay to lie to me?"

"I didn't lie, I omitted," I point out, but it's a stupid move and I know it.

"So why did it end? And where is she now?" she asks, arms folded tightly across her chest, her foot tapping irately.

I search her eyes. She doesn't know that Lianna is my ex-wife. She hasn't put two and two together *yet*, and for whatever reason, Trey hasn't mentioned it to her. It puts me in a very precarious situation. If I lie now and say I have no idea where she is, there is no coming back from that.

"It ended because she screwed Trey behind my back," I say, hoping this will deflect her attention for long enough for me to think.

It does.

"Humph, figured," she mutters.

"It angered me more than usual because she didn't even know it wasn't me," I add.

"More than usual? He's done it before?"

"A dozen times. He always wants what I have."

She squints at me. "She really didn't know? And that was her defense?"

"Yes," I say, glad we are talking about this and not the other thing.

"Have you ever done it to him?" She asks an insightful question that I can't avoid.

"I won't lie to you. Yes, I have. It was a game when we were younger, before I got married. He crossed a line by taking my wife. I *will not* let that happen again."

She nods thoughtfully.

Just as I think she has forgotten her other question, she asks, "So where is she now?"

I shrug. "Who cares?" I say. I mean, I told her to fuck off. She could be anywhere *right now*.

"Do you still love her?" she asks quietly.

"Absolutely not. I didn't even love her to begin with. At least not in the way that I know love now. I thought I loved her, but after I met you and fell in love with you, I knew that I had never been in love before. Not even with her."

"Is there anything else I should know?" she asks.

This is my chance, my one and only chance to come completely clean about everything. Lianna, Blayne, that I am half Light Fae, about the deal I struck with Trey after Dad unbound our powers.

"No," I say and pull her to me as she smiles and tilts her head back for a kiss.

43

~PRES~

I storm into our bedroom, shaking with fury. I can't believe what I just saw. I need to find Delinda and tell her.

I stop dead when I see Rex standing in the bedroom, staring out of the window.

My heart thumps and I slam the door closed, causing him to turn and give me an inquiring look.

"You absolute fuck!" I roar at him, approaching him quickly, my hand bunched into a fist. I draw back and before I know what I am doing, I punch him in the face, breaking his nose.

"Fuck!" he roars back at me, clutching at his face, blood gushing everywhere, until it heals. "What the fuck, you prick!"

"How dare you! How can you even stand in here after what you've done?"

He glares at me. I'm panting with rage, exacerbated by his sheer audacity. He sniffs and wipes the last of the blood from his nose with the back of his hand. "Some left hook you've got there, kid," he drawls. "Want to tell me what bit you on the ass?"

"You know what you did," I snarl at him and look around. "Where is Delinda?"

"She isn't here," he replies, gesturing around. "And what did I do?"

"Ugh," I spit out at him. He can't even admit it, even though I saw him with my own eyes, he is going to stand there and deny it. "I know everything," I add, giving him a death stare.

He tilts his head at me, eyes narrowed. "Oh?" he asks, playing coy. "What's that then?"

I shake my head at him. "You don't deserve to have her love you."

"Now, wait just a damn minute," he growls at me. "How dare you come in here, punch me in the face, insult me and then tell me I'm not good enough for our wife. Who the fuck do you think you are?"

"The man that loves her," I growl back. "*You* are a fucking liar and a cheat! And I am going to make sure that Delinda knows all about you as soon as I find her."

His eyes flash dangerously at me, but I don't give a shit. He is the one that is in the wrong here. He is the one that kissed another woman. He is the one that has betrayed Delinda's love and trust with some cheap slut.

"Was it worth it?" I taunt him. "Was it worth losing Delinda over? Because I will make sure she has nothing to do with you after she finds out what I have to tell her. I will un-link you from the tie-to-life spell and help her kick you to your flaming death!"

"Wow," he says, looking surprised. "You've got some anger issues there, Pres. Look, I don't know what you think I did, but I can guarantee you that T…"

"Save it," I spit out. "I don't want to hear another word from you."

"Pres, it wasn't…"

"I SAID SAVE IT!" I thunder at him, bunching my hands into fists again.

"What the devil is going on in here?" To'Kah asks, bursting in. "I can hear you yelling from down the hall."

"Rex is a fucking asshole that has betrayed our wife and I am going to fucking kill him!" I launch myself at him, but To'Kah grabs me by my collar, stopping me in mid-air. I growl and kick out, scrabbling to get free but, to my utter disgust, I find myself several inches off the ground seeing that To'Kah has a height advantage over me, and most men as it happens, of about half a foot.

Fucker.

"Slow down, tiger," To'Kah says to me. "Start at the beginning."

"No, I am done with him," I say petulantly, kicking out, but getting nowhere near the Judas. "I want to find Delinda and make sure she knows all about him."

"What did you do to aggravate the kid?" To'Kah asks Rex, ignoring me completely.

"Rah!" I cry, still struggling in mid-air.

Rex shrugs. "He won't say, but I am sure it has to do with my evil…"

"You are evil," I yell at him. "An evil bastard!"

"Fuck's sake!" he roars back at me. "Stop interrupting me, you little asshole."

To'Kah is jiggling me about due to the laughter that is bubbling up and out of him, and then he drops me on my feet. "Evil?" he prompts Rex.

"Twin," Rex says, and it stops my advance in its tracks.

"Liar," I hiss. "Your father sent Trey away and he wouldn't dare show his face back here after what he did."

"Wanna bet?" Rex drawls. "The nerve of that prick still astounds me." He heaves a massive sigh. "What did he do?"

I gape at him like a goldfish, my anger deflating as quickly as it rose up. Of course it was Trey. I should've known, but I really didn't think he would come back here, especially seeing as the Chosen bond was severed. I jumped to the wrong conclusion and betrayed my friend.

"I saw him kissing another woman. A blonde, someone I've not seen around here before. I thought it was you," I say to Rex, but I won't apologize. If he knew Trey was here, he should have told us immediately.

I give him a defiant glare as his face goes dark. "You think that I would do that to my wife?" he asks so quietly; it is far more menacing than if he had yelled at me.

"I did, yes," I say stubbornly, sticking my chin up.

"Oh, kid, you don't know fuck all about me, do you? There is a special place next to Hell's Castle for those that cheat. I have been burned by that act, by my own fucking brother, no less, so I can assure you that I would never put someone that I love as much as I love Delinda, through that. Quite apart from the fact THAT I LOVE HER!" he bellows in my face.

"Where was this?" To'Kah asks, remaining calm in the face of Rex's rage at me.

Okay, so I admit to being a bit of an ass, but I had cause.

"In Delly's office," I say quietly. "I'm sorry, Rex, I got so angry, I assumed it was you, but I should have known better."

"Whatever," he snarls at me. "I'm just glad that you found me first and not Delinda. If you had told her that, she would've suffered needlessly."

I nod, agreeing with that. I would've caused her pain for no reason. But then time slows down.

We look at each other in horror as we realize that this is set-up, only not for me, but for Delly.

44

~DELINDA~

I land on a cliff-top far away from the Fortress. I needed to fly; to clear my head after the conversation with Rex. I am reassured that he doesn't care about his ex-wife anymore, but I have no idea what *her* intentions are. He dumped her after she cheated with Trey, so she probably has unresolved feelings for him. I fold my wings and stare out over my Empire.

My fucking Empire.

I still can't believe that I did this. I claimed the throne and fulfilled my destiny. I have an heir on the way to pass all of this along to. I wonder if he or she will have any Fae in them. It is a strong possibility. I hope that To'Kah doesn't suggest we bind their powers because I won't do it.

The bond that I share with my husbands pings. They are anxious about something, wanting to find me, but I am not ready to go back to them yet. I am enjoying this solitude. I erect a simple cloaking spell so that they can't find me. It's horrible of me, but my head needs the quiet for a bit. I am convinced that Lianna is, in fact, Rex's ex-wife. Her appearance here at the same time as Trey's is just too much of a coincidence. I gave him the opportunity to tell me and he didn't. I don't know why he chose to lie to me, but he did and that hurts me. I need time to figure out my next move in regard to him. I *am* sure that he doesn't love her anymore, but that leaves a dozen more reasons why he didn't tell me it was her.

I huff out a breath, watching as the thin stream of smoke wisps away on the breeze.

Dusk is falling. I'll have to go back to my husbands soon. They are probably fretting now that they can't sense me or find me.

I step back from the cliff edge and start the Shift.

I stretch my back out a few minutes later as I stand naked and a bit chilly. The sudden gust of wind puckers my nipples enticingly. I reach up to tweak them, twisting them and wincing from the pain. My advancing pregnancy is playing all sorts of havoc on my body. I run my hands over my breasts and down over my tiny bump.

I smile serenely and turn my face into the breeze. My hair flies away from my face and I sigh. I Astral on a long, green dress, pulling the sleeves down over my wrists. I have gone cold, but I want to feel it.

I sit on the precipice of the cliff, dangling my feet over the edge. I look down. I can't even see the ravine floor it is that far down. I find peace this high up, knowing that I am alone.

"What am I going to do about you?" I ask out loud. I am tired of secrets, but I am also tired of confrontation. Whatever reasons Rex has for failing to tell me about Lianna, must be good ones. He wouldn't risk so much out of a triviality. But what they are, only he knows. I want to trust him, trust that he will come to me in his own time to tell me, but at the same time, I outright asked him if there was anything else I needed to know, and he lied.

I decide that it all falls on her. Rex doesn't love her anymore, but maybe *she* can tell me why he is keeping her a secret. Perhaps a conversation with her, wife to ex-wife, is in order. Or, better yet, Empress to subject. That will cause her more consternation and hopefully force her into telling me the truth.

I stand up and Astral out, back to the Fortress, intent on my plan. I keep the cloak in place, as I still don't want my husbands to find me.

I hurry to find Aida. If anyone can tell me where Lianna is right now, she can.

I find her lingering in the foyer, her eyes darting around for signs of trouble. It makes me wonder, for a moment, how Trey and Lianna got in here in the first place. Surely, they should have been stopped. But that is a problem for another time. I want to speak with Lianna. I need to find out what the Hell she is doing here and what she wants with Rex. Does she want him back or is she here merely to cause trouble with Trey?

Either way, I intend to find out.

"Aida," I call out.

She turns to me, not seeing me, but able to hear me.

"Dammit," I mutter and lift the cloaking spell a fraction. It's a risk in case my husbands can find me. I need to be quick or Rex will stop me, I have absolutely no doubt about that.

Her eyes widen slightly, but she says nothing, which doesn't surprise me in the least.

"I need to find someone. A woman who came here today. Blonde..." I trail off as I see, out of the corner of my eye, the woman I am searching for, disappear down one of the corridors to my left. "Never mind," I mutter and resume the cloaking spell.

I scamper off after her, following her into the corridor and seeing her long blonde hair swish around a corner.

Where is she going in such a hurry?

Bend after bend, I trail behind her, wanting to see where she is going before I confront her.

My blood turns cold when I see her heading towards the steps to the outside terrace where I first engaged with Rex.

Did she used to meet him up there as well? Was it *their* place before it became ours? My stomach drops, but I follow her anyway. I need to see with my own eyes if she is meeting Rex up there.

I take the steps slowly, one at a time, refraining from racing into a potentially devastating scenario.

I reach the top of the steps and peek around the door. I see Lianna in a sexy clinch with my husband, their mouths devouring each other, as their hands fumble with their clothes.

I gulp, but then take in a deep breath and the rational side of my brain screams at me. It's Trey. It has to be. I can't feel any bond, but I have cloaked myself, blocking anything from going out as well as coming in. But it's Trey. It has to be. I can't fall for this trick, or whatever it is.

I stare at them for a moment longer, convinced, despite his lies, that Rex wouldn't do this to me, especially here. I turn away, the sight of them still making me nauseous as it shows me exactly what this bitch looks like with Rex. A mental picture I would rather *not* have, thank you very much. My conversation with her can wait. Right now, I need to find Rex, make sure that he is as far away from this woman as he can get.

I am about to Astral off when his moaned words stop me dead in my tracks. "Oh, Little Dragon, I have missed you so much."

What?

I turn back to them slowly, the bile rising in my throat again.

Little Dragon? *Little Dragon*? LittleDragon. LittleDragon. LittleDragon.

No, I must've heard him wrong. It is my overactive imagination playing tricks on me. Isn't it?

"Call me that again," she murmurs. "I have missed hearing it from your lips, my love."

I watch as he grins down at her. "Little Dragon," he whispers to her, brushing her hair away from her face.

She gasps and clutches him to her, wrapping her legs around him when he lifts her up and slams her against the Fortress wall, right next to the hole he made with his fist when I told him I wanted to bring To'Kah into our marriage.

They fumble with their clothes. He rips her dress from her neckline down over her breasts in his urgency to grab at her tits.

"Little Dragon," he pants as she gets his cock free.

"Again!" she cries.

"Little Dragon, I love you!" He impales her on his cock, her cries of ecstasy echoing off the high wall of the Fortress and against the cliff-sides opposite the terrace.

"No," I sob, the tears falling even though I don't want them to. "No, it's not. It's not. It's not Rex."

But that is what Rex calls me. What Trey *didn't* call me so that I knew he wasn't Rex.

My heart explodes with the pain of seeing my husband screwing his ex-wife in our special place.

My cloaking spell drops in my anguish; I feel the rush of emotions hitting me and in the next second To'Kah and Pres are behind me.

"Delly!" Pres cries, taking in the sight before us. "Don't..."

"Ah," I cry out, falling into his arms, as To'Kah grabs my hand.

"It's not Rex. It's Trey," he rushes to say.

"No, no, it's Rex," I insist, my voice shaking with my sorrow. I know what I heard.

"Delinda," Rex says to me, appearing next To'Kah. "Princess." He takes my hand from To'Kah, pulling me to him. "Look into my eyes. You know it's me. You know that I would never betray you."

I do look at him. I glance back at the couple still fucking, not even caring that we are standing here watching them, apparently.

I look back at Rex, but don't say anything because he *has* betrayed me by lying to me about her.

"Princess," he warns me. "Don't let him get in between us."

"It isn't him," I spit out. "I know she is your ex. You lied."

"Ah," he says, sheepishly. "I wanted to tell you, but…"

"Save it," I bark at him. Now that he is here in front of me and not behind me with another woman, any relief I first felt has vanished. I am so pissed with him I could beat him to death with my bare hands. "You lied. I asked you if there was anything else, I needed to know, and you lied."

"I know," he says soothingly. "I didn't want you anywhere near her. I wanted to get rid of her."

"Scared we will compare notes?" I ask scathingly.

"No, I just don't want her in our home, rubbing what we used to have in your face. And I certainly don't want *this*!" He gestures to Trey and Lianna, who have finally reached the end of their rendezvous. "I will deal with you later!" Rex snarls at his twin, before he looks back at me. "Please, Delinda. You have to trust me."

"No, I really don't," I say and without thinking it through entirely, I Astral off back to Earth, to my parent's home in Buckinghamshire, England.

As soon as my feet hit the ground, I throw up another cloaking spell. But it's too late Rex has already followed me.

"I don't want to talk to you," I say, dropping the spell a fraction so that I can yell at him to go away, but not have anyone else turning up.

"That's rude," he says, approaching me with an arrogant smirk.

I cast a hard look at him. He is dressed in a glowing white and gold suit, the orbs of the Fae dancing around his head.

My heart thumps in my chest. "Who are you?" I ask. I know for definite that this isn't Rex now because he is Light Fae, that much is blindingly obvious, and Rex isn't Fae. But this man has Rex's face, his hard, sexy body, his arrogant attitude.

"No," I say as a wild theory starts to develop in my head. "Oh no!" I stamp my foot.

"Oh, yes, Princess," he says, that smile of Rex's that makes me wet as Hell, passing across his face for an instant before he goes serious. "It is my honor to finally meet you. I didn't think you would ever come out of the Dragon Realms."

Shit.

I have left the sanctuary of my home and landed right in the lap of my Fae mate. But somehow, he looks exactly like Rex and that can mean only one thing. This man is what Trey can bring to the table. A third brother to fulfill my triplet fantasy; the fantasy that I only made up to insult him.

"I am Blayne," he says, now standing right in front of me.

I look up at him and practical drool on his shoes. Not only does he look just like my husband, a man that I find so gorgeous it hurts my eyes sometimes to look at him, but he also knows me better than I would care to admit. He has been inside my head for weeks now, talking to me, knowing my innermost thoughts.

"That's right, Princess," he croons, curling my hair behind my ear. "I am your destiny."

Shit.

Fuck.

What the Hell am I supposed to do now?

The End

Stay Tuned for Book 3 of the Dragon Realms Series – Coming Early 2020!

ABOUT THE AUTHOR

EVE NEWTON

Eve is a British novelist with a specialty for paranormal romance, with strong female leads, causing her to develop a Reverse Harem Fantasy series, several years ago: The Forever Series.

She lives in the UK, with her husband and four kids, so finding the time to write is short, but definitely sweet. She currently has two on-going series, with a number of spin-offs in the making. Eve hopes to release some new and exciting projects in the next couple of years, so stay tuned!

Start Eve's Reverse Harem Fantasy Series, with the first two books in the Forever Series as a double edition!

Newsletter Sign up for exclusive content and giveaways:
https://emailoctopus.com/lists/a0f1e6a3-7a21-11e9-9307-06b4694bee2a/forms/subscribe

Facebook Reader Group: https://www.facebook.com/groups/2042198485818170

Facebook: http://facebook.com/evenewtonforever

Twitter: https://twitter.com/AuthorEve

Website: https://evenewtonauthor.com/

OTHER BOOKS BY EVE NEWTON

The Forever Series:

Forever & The Power of One: Double Edition

Revelations

Choices

The Ties That Bind

Trials

Switch & The Other Switch

Secrets

Betrayal

Sacrifice

Conflict & Obsession: Double Edition

Wrath

Revenge

Changes & Forever After: Double Edition

Arathia

Constantine

The Dragon Heiress (Delinda's Story)

The Dragon Realms Series:

The Dragon Heiress

Claiming the Throne

Circle of Darkness:

Wild Hearts: Book One

Savage Love: Book Two

Tainted Blood: Book Three

Darkest Desires: Book Four

The Early Years Series:

Aefre & Constantine 1 & 2

The Bound Series:

Demon Bound

Demon Freed

Demon Returned

Enchained Hearts Series:

Lives Entwined

Lives Entangled

Made in the USA
Las Vegas, NV
29 September 2021